The Great Eight Chase

by

Fabian Grant

Paperback edition first published in the United Kingdom in 2023 by aSys Publishing

Hardback edition first published in the United Kingdom in 2023 by aSys Publishing

eBook edition first published in the United Kingdom in 2023 by aSys Publishing

Disclaimer

This is a work of fiction. Names, characters, businesses, places, events and incidents are either the products of the author's imagination or used in a fictitious manner. Any resemblance to actual persons, living or dead, or actual events is purely coincidental.

ISBN: 978-1-913438-73-9

aSys Publishing 2023

http://www.asys-publishing.co.uk

Books available

The Greenhouse

The Kids That Never Quit

The Great Eight Chase

Welcome to Winterberry High

We're Not So Different

The Golden Oldies Strike Back

The Night Santa Forgot

Game Over

They're special breeds ruling the racing nation
But money and greed is a bad combination
(No animals were hurt during the writing of this book)

Catch Me If You Can
Instagram - mrfabiangrant
Twitter - @fabiangrant3
&
Don't forget to review on
Goodreads .com

CONTENTS

CHAPTER 1

Gambling

Gambling: they'll simply tell you it's a mug's game. And I'd tend to agree. Punters flock in droves to fork over their hard-earned cash. All to see their favourite horses and sport teams crash and burn, costing them a fortune. Gambling's one of the very worst creations, unless you're a bookie that is, which I'm fortunate to be.

See, us bookies have it covered from all angles and the money keeps rolling in. I'll give you odds on two cockroaches racing through a pile of sick. You name it, as long as there's a winner, I'll take it. We get a bad reputation in the media for being evil, drawing poor people in with multiple offers. But I feel we give lower-income families the opportunity to make a quick buck. In fact, I think us bookies should be praised.

How about a round of applause for your local bookmaker?

No, suit yourself. Love us or hate us, my bank manager worships the ground I walk on. He'll bow, perform a curtsy. I'm sure he'd streak naked through Trafalgar Square if I asked. Maybe on my next appointment we'll see.

Our service at Bet Your Life On It is to allow you the glory of winning without the hard work. It's like getting a championship medal from the comfort of your own home. Still not convinced? There's just no pleasing some people.

I'm absolutely not money orientated. For instance, last summer I offered customers one pound free bets for every hundred quid spent and lost. A heart made from sweet candy, I know. Fancy a punt yet? Come on, you know you wanna. You work all week, then let off a bit of steam, drop a couple quid on Man United at odds of four hundred to one on. Meaning you put four hundred pounds in to receive the princely sum of one pound. Can't say fairer than that can we? It's still a profit.

Here at Bet Your Life On It we aim to enhance your betting experience. We've got comfy swivel lounge chairs; giant flat screen 3D tellies, surround sound of course. Wouldn't be doing my civic duty if I didn't make punters feel at the races, would I?

After all, the customers come first, except when they're gambling. LOL.

I've owned my bookmakers for twenty-five glorious successful years. We've had some startling highs: James 'Buster' Douglas' shock knockout of 'Iron' Mike Tyson certainly brings a smile to my face and a glint to my eye.

However, nothing lasts forever and while I was riding a wave of complete prosperity gaining riches, the landscapes of worldwide betting transformed in one devastating blow. I'm getting to my story in a few shakes of a lamb's tail. Just bear with me. Talking in detail about a single race that destroyed bookmakers for eternity hurts.

I don't expect sympathy from you. I see you're not there yet. Maybe if you spoke to a client of mine? Mr Reynolds was one of my regular punters; each and every day I've helped him make sound investments on greyhounds, horses and a variety of other sports. Hey, what's a pension for? He's ninety-one years young; because I appreciate him so much, on his birthday my present is one fifty pee bet on odds of forty to one or higher. Bet small, win big.

At 10.30 a.m., he'd arrive without fail. I made it 10.29. Knock! Knock! His frail figure loomed, his peaked old man cap drenched in rain.

"Are you opening? I'm feeling extra lucky. Had that dream about a jockey all in white again," his wee brittle voice said.

Many gambling addicts have silly superstitions, from a rabbit's foot to idiotic dreams. I knew one bloke who'd only gamble on Thursdays between six and seven in a cream suit for some profound reason. Oh well, each to their own.

"Sadly, Mr Reynolds, we've closed down."

"What? No, I've got a dead cert in the Cherry Town hurdles," he explained.

I unlocked the door, letting him inside from the soaking rain. It took him some time – with the hip and knee replacements he was more metal than human.

"All betting has been suspended indefinitely."

He placed his overcoat on a peg. As we eventually age, nobody stays young forever; our physical skills get worse, wear and tear you see. Mr Reynolds' eardrums have spent a lifetime of hearing loud bangs. He is a survivor of world wars. We'll cut him a little slack.

"Sorry, what did you say?" he asked.

"All betting is off, from online poker to sports."

Mr Reynolds looked glum, his eyes dropping with sadness. I personally believe that gambling was the only thing that brought him joy, preventing him from kicking the bucket.

"But gambling is the only hobby I enjoy. I'll be at a total loss now. Where else can you put a quid in and walk away four grand the better? Suppose I'll probably go home and get old and lonely, just waiting to kick the bucket," he said, sounding at an all-time low.

"You'll find another hobby. How about bowls?" I suggested.

He sneezed. With his slowed reactions a tissue didn't control the spray. Nose fluid dripped, leaking onto my tiled floor. "Bowls! I'm not dead yet, I love bookies; the banter, the uncertainty of odds on favourites failing. The big derby upsets." You could feel the passion.

"We bookmakers took a massive hit on that corrupt horse race last week, we all went belly up."

"Come on, one lousy showing can't demolish a whole betting market."

4

The Great Eight Chase

On most occasions, even an entire awful week wouldn't break our banks. Most betting companies make tremendous profits during down times like the end of the footy season or the winter when the ground's too tough for horses and greyhounds alike.

"They bled me dry. Took us all by surprise. Still can't get my head around it, never seen a finish like it."

Mr Reynolds was intrigued by the demise of a gambling network so flushed in riches; something major had to have happened.

"Tell me more, how did it happen?" His eyes lit up.

"Pain's too deep, cuts like a sword Mr Reynolds. My business and lifestyle disappeared from under me."

"Don't leave me hanging. I deserve to know what cost me my favourite pastime."

There I slouched in silence, unsure whether I felt stable enough to discuss a matter so dear to my heart.

"It would shock and disgust you if I explained how my demise unfolded."

The old man cracked a smile. What beautiful gums he had.

"I've been around the block a fair few times. You can't get up early enough in the morning to catch me out," he wisely stated.

"All due respect, Mr Reynolds, this story will knock your socks off."

He disputed my notion, shaking his head. "Ninety-one years says I've seen and done many things. Nothing can rattle me."

A sudden gust of wind floated through the room, knocking his brown walking stick off its peg.

"Jeepers," he screamed.

"Thought you said you never get rattled," I winked.

"My hearing aid magnifies sounds." He began taking shallow breaths.

I helped him to a seat near the counter.

"Shall I call an ambulance?"

Mr Reynolds' face kept changing colour: white, pink, dark pink, red and then dark red. I was obviously concerned. Gotta look after the old ones.

"Feel a bit woozy, let me get my bearings."

I ran to the kitchen, fetching him a glass of water.

"Haven't you got anything stronger? I did have a major episode," he asked.

"Sure you can handle it?"

"I been drinking spirits since a wee grasshopper, my father gave me my first tipple of gin in a sippy cup." (Never recommended!)

I went into my secret stash, picking out my finest brand of gin.

"Nice, very nice." Mr Reynolds snatched the bottle, tipping out the liquid.

Something told me he hadn't got the greatest relationship with alcohol. As he poured his lips began to wobble and his eyes dilated, completely concentrated on the bottle. It was like he was willing the liquid into the glass before launching the gin into his mouth.

"Steady on man, savour the flavour, want some ice?" I instructed him.

"Please, ice. Ice! Ice?" he looked at me, disgusted.

Mr Reynolds knocked one back after another. Soon we were on a second bottle. The thing about alcohol is too much of it can make you very, very talkative.

"So let it rip. Rip it up. Share your story with me, explain how Britain's biggest bookies ended up broke," he rocked and rolled.

"Another day, it's late already."

"Nonsense, just gone noon. I demand you tell me every last detail, buddy."

I took a swift drink, probably my sixth or erm . .. sixth, or what's after sixth? Silly me, eighth. I slammed the glass against the wall. Alcohol makes you do weird things. Don't drink, kids.

"I'm not budging until you open up," he pestered.

"Fine, this tale will dazzle your mind like no other," I conceded.

The wise old man smiled. "What odds would you give me?"

"Odds for what?" I asked, confused.

He locked eyes with me. "Odds that I won't be astonished."

Life's full of gambles; some gambles pay off tenfold. Others, however, seem too dicey. "Thousand to one, very special circumstances," I said, confident he'd bite.

"Well, fantastic. Fifty quid sounds fair."

Fifty quid at a thousand to one? That's fifty K. Now usually a bet of this enormity would go to head office. Fortunately a race as crazy as the Great Eight Chase happens once and never again.

CHAPTER 2

Mr & Mrs Brown

What do you actually know about racehorses? Not too much, right? They're slightly larger than the average horse and significantly smaller than a giraffe. I guess they're quite quick as well. Other than that? Oh yes, they have tails.

Horse racing has been with us for donkey's years; it has a long history steeped in tradition. An elite crop of thorough-bred stallions rally over a course, being whipped by jockeys for the enjoyment of millions of viewers, and they call it a sport. Nevertheless, it's not for me to judge. I'd be a bit of a hypocrite since I made a sensational living from gambling. When the business of horse racing began, small owners used to take their steeds out to local events and tracks, wagering friendly bets. As with everything, bigger is always better. Better tracks, bigger horses to larger winning fees. Soon horseracing wasn't a friendly way of competing animal versus animal. The game transformed to a world of dog eat dog. Horses were no longer looked at as giant pets, but sound investments. One you could literally ride to a pot of gold.

The Great Eight Chase

Make no mistake; raising horses is no easy business. The cost can be extraordinary. So think twice before asking mummy and daddy for that Shetland pony; it could wind up being your Christmas and birthday present for the next fifteen years. Found that out the hard way. Vet bills, feeding costs, stables and stable maintenance. Tinkerbell cost me an arm and a leg. Not to mention you only recoup your stake if he or she wins. Which isn't often; some horses go a career without winning a single race. I love those animals and here's why. When a rubbish racer loses continuously, I as a bookmaker shoot his odds up through the roof. It'll tempt stupid punters into a cheeky pound bet. Some might say I'm stealing, whereas I feel it's educating. If it sounds too good to be true, it probably is.

Success brings money and money breeds greedy people. And predictably the super rich make it their very own adult playground, throwing out lavish sums of money willy nilly. Honestly I believe the multibillionaires felt their horses were an extension of themselves. In fact, some of these rich people started to look like their noble pets. The long nose, flared nostrils, bulging stomachs, massive teeth and big heads that look down on poorer folks. Became difficult to tell them apart; both flapped their gums, chatting nonsense.

The track is where races start and finish, winners and losers, fortunes lost and found. Surprise endings and fairytale stories all develop on racecourses everywhere around the world. Jockeys and steeds working as one competing for the ultimate prize of victory, I'll never forgive those rotten animals. Ruined it for us all, well, me and the deluded punters.

Easily the best courses reside in the capital of England. And the capital of England is? E of course but for the sake of this story we'll say it's London. The nation's capital controlled major racing forever. Big city lights brought Europe's first-class participants to London. French, Italian and Spanish stallions were carted over by ferry to grace UK-based tracks. The one thing I realised about people in my line of work is that the more exotic the name, the more people will spend. A Spanish horse called Segundo en el Mejor generated a killing; its translation means 'second at best'. Also, an Italian one titled Niente di Speciale produced dud performance after dud performance. His name meant 'nothing special'.

Whilst the south enjoyed the glitz and showbusiness of monstrous events, up north was a whole different kettle of fish. Manchester, in some areas considered the London of the north, was struggling. Each and every racetrack lay dead. Tumbleweed blew across the damp dull sand. Stands were broken and cracked, metal railings unkempt and covered with rust. Hurdle hedges outgrew their barriers, uprooting the turf. Racing up north was as good as dead.

Until one fateful man, on a winter Monday morning, had a bright idea in his dim-witted mind. Mr Brown, as we shall call him to protect his identity, owned a farm. And on that farm he had some . . . oh forget about it. Mr Brown adored farm life – rearing crops and animals was a personal favourite of his. A combine harvester became his companion and weapon of choice. While fertilising the ground he'd tell anyone who'd listen about grain tank capacity, straw walkers and bottom sieves. Complete gobbledygook to me as well.

"Are you coming inside, love?" his wife would ask daily.

"No, gotta give the old girl a service, then I'll wash her stone traps."

"Do you love that machine more than me?"

There was an echoing wind as Mr Brown contemplated her question. I mean the harvester kept churning out spectacular results on a regular basis, making him feel like a king, unlike his wife.

"Excuse me, I said do you love that horrible machine more than me?" she barked.

"Don't speak about her that way." Mr Brown covered her headlamps, supposedly protecting her ears. So, so incredibly sad.

I'm sure Mr Brown, to this day, still misses his brilliant tractor, motoring over the green fields in a world of his own.

Sad he couldn't just stay on his farm. Then again, wouldn't make much of a story if he did.

Large supermarket chains had swallowed up local independent farmers. Mr Brown was now on their hit list. Letters upon letters came through the post offering ludicrous amounts of cash for his land. Steadily the sums increased, but Mr Brown was one stubborn bugger.

"That's a lot of money on the table," smiled Mrs Brown.

Mr Brown lifted the envelope, peeking at half a dozen zeros. "Money can't buy you happiness love."

"Soon they'll price us out of the market anyway and we'll have to sell this place at a lower price."

"But this farm is my kingdom."

He'd sometimes park his combine harvester outside his bedroom window, so it was the first thing he saw in the morning.

A couple of weeks went by without a single letter. Mr Brown assumed the big bad supermarket realised he wouldn't dance to their tune. Not entirely; supermarket empires aren't built in days and definitely don't take no for an answer.

"See love, you show them resistance, they back off, like all bullies," Mr Brown said, kissing his wife before leaving for another day of farming.

He had supplied regional restaurants and care homes with organic fruit and veg for years. It was stuff like this that made him love the job; making an impact in the local community. The Grub Hub was one of his biggest customers. He'd drive his van five miles to deliver his goods on Tuesdays.

When he reached The Grub Hub, a supervisor met him at the entrance. Sporting a new uniform, in the silk black shirt and trouser ensemble he looked quite snazzy.

"Greetings my man," said Mr Brown, holding a clipboard with an invoice attached.

"Mr Brown, how is farm life treating you?" he replied.

"Can't complain, keeping my head above water. Where do you want the goods?"

The supervisor wavered. He struggled to keep eye contact with Mr Brown, and his pores opened with sweat.

"Er . . . About that Mr Brown, I tried to call, but your wife told me you left already."

"Had to get out the house. You know how women can be?"

They shared a sly smile; couldn't think why.

Up north the weather can change in an instant, and peaky white clouds brought a suffocating icy wind.

"What's it you want to talk about, doubling your supply? No wait, let me guess, tripling it, or start paying me extra."

The supervisor didn't switch emotion in response to any of Mr Brown's joking suggestions. A stern look glossed his face throughout.

"It's with great regret I inform you I no longer require your services. I'm sorry."

Mr Brown's heart sunk. One of his prime customers deserting him set alarm bells ringing.

"If it's price, I can cut you a better discount, since you're so appreciated." If you listened closely, you'd hear massive levels of sorrow.

"Price isn't an issue," said the supervisor compassionately.

"Well, what then?"

The man shot a glance at the sun as if the answers were somewhere in its rays. "Those details are off limits to some-one of my standing, manager's not back till Thursday."

Mr Brown huffed as the young man hurried inside. A pattern began forming among his clients; they told false poxy stories. One even tried to convince him he didn't use vegetables anymore. Another acted like he'd never seen Mr Brown in his life and threatened to call the police.

Something funny was happening. A bigger party was squeezing Mr Brown's customer base. That night he returned home with a truck loaded with veg. Miserable and slightly depressed he went off to bed, ignoring his wife.

As dawn broke on a new day, the postman walked up the driveway. I'm a poet and I just don't know it, oh wait yeah I do. The postman (who was actually a woman) pushed two envelopes through the letterbox.

Mr Brown came downstairs unshaven and unwashed.

"Sleepyhead, you haven't slept past six in ten years," said a worried Mrs Brown.

"Is that the mail wifey?" he huffed.

She handed him both envelopes, which contained their fate, but which one would he choose?

CHAPTER 3

The Letters

Mr and Mrs Brown sat around the kitchen table. A hearty breakfast of steaming hot cornmeal porridge was dished out in big bowls. Mrs Brown was a wizard with porridge; she'd smooth out all the lumps, sprinkling on a few almonds for decoration and taste.

They stared at each envelope as if they were filled with poison.

"You open them," said Mr Brown, shoving the letters to her.

"No, they're addressed to the homeowner," she responded.

"We both know I'm not the leader here."

He was correct; Mrs Brown ran the farmhouse. While her husband ploughed the fields, she kept things in order.

"Well, as leader, I command you to open them."

"Fine, we'll open one each."

Mr Brown went first, being 'the man of the house'. A reaction like his couldn't be described or drawn. The letter unfolded like this.

Dear Mr Brown,

As you may or may not be aware – can't tell if those tractor fumes have gotten to your dumb brain – your regular clients have cast you to one side in favour of a bigger prize; me and my supermarket. They'll never take supplies off some jumped-up small-time average farmer. I mean, you idiot. I'm sure you're now scrambling around diving into a certain piggybank, looking for old coppers to keep the lights on. Never play games with a supermarket. Super's in the title, fool. But it's not all bad news; I'm still willing to buy your property for one pound if you stay on as farmer. See I've heard rave reviews about your farming techniques. In fact I had lunch at The Grub Hub. You know The Grub Hub? Of course you know, look who I'm talking to. Anyway, their vegetable medley was fantastic. Whatever you're doing definitely works. I'd hate to see a talent like yourself lose your way. Nice talking, hope to hear from you soon.

Yours sincerely,

Mr Moneybags

"Those beeping beepers, they're beeping beepers. I'll beep them until the beeping end. What the beeping beep do they take me for?" Mr Brown blazed.

His temper overspilled as he flipped the kitchen table, splashing wonderful cornmeal porridge up the walls.

"What does it say?" asked Mrs Brown.

The horrible letter made him so angry he couldn't speak, and he could never read the words aloud.

Mrs Brown looked over it. "At least they used sincerely."

"Bleeding fatcat companies squashing people like insects, it's disgusting," he blew.

"No point getting all worked up," she said, taking a damp cloth to the cornmeal-covered walls.

"They're dirty swine, I'll refuse to sell."

"Listen, cool off and then we'll discuss our options," she reasoned.

Mr Brown was a raging hothead. He furiously grabbed his coat and the keys to his combine harvester.

"Where are you going love?"

"Show them a small-time farmer. I'm a fool am I? We'll see about that," he mumbled.

He stormed out the back door, heading straight for his fondest machine.

"Now what honey?"

"I'm replying to their letter, harvester style. Clean-up on aisle three, four and five." He checked the fuel levels and tyre pressure before entering the cab.

"Stop, you're insane," she begged.

"I didn't want it to come to this but my hands are tied. First I'm gonna make an appearance at Mr Moneybags' supermarket, make a few adjustments to their entrance. Then if I feel peckish maybe I'll drop in on The Grub Hub, see what's on the menu," he laughed.

"You'll be arrested! Sent to prison for damaging public property and endangering human life."

"So they pushed me past breaking point."

Mrs Brown knew her husband was a very passionate man and had an 'act first, think later' mentality.

"They'll confiscate the combine, lock it up in an impound lot. Then she'll be sold off or crushed."

Mr Brown unclenched his fist, relaxing slightly. Visions of some hideous greasy farmer owning his precious combine harvester brought him back to normality. He parked the machine back in its barn.

"Shall we call the number? It's just an opening offer."

"Over my dead body will they buy my land," he huffed, putting an icepack on his head.

"Hope you have another idea."

Mr Brown felt trapped between his integrity and finances.

"Well, there are a lot of bills racking up for a farm of this size," she said.

"I know woman. I know." With his stress increasing, he opened letter number two.

Why?

Dear Sir or Madam,

I personally hope everything is well. I've been feeling generous. How would you like some extra money? Help you with your piling debts. I can be of some assistance. Enclosed is a free £10 voucher; just type in the promotional code on our website and enjoy. We have a range of greyhounds, football, basketball, horse racing and a host of other sports as well as specials. Our odds are phenomenal and can't be matched or beaten, here at 'Bet Your Life On It', the bookies you certainly can trust.

Kind regards

Bet Your Life On It

Mrs Brown glanced at the voucher. "Stupid junk mail, I told them no more. Pass it here, I'll chuck it in the bin."

"No, hold on," Mr Brown removed his icepack, sitting up. He stared, fascinated, at the racehorse displayed on the voucher. Something was clicking.

"You're not seriously thinking of gambling, it's an awful habit," hissed Mrs Brown.

"Not directly. If my theory works we'll be rich for eternity."

There was a glazed shine to his eyes as ideas floated into orbit.

"I'm gonna build a racetrack so marvellous, people will pay money to watch the grass being cut."

Pretty bold statement for a man in a relationship with a tractor, but hey, everyone has to dream.

"Right, I'm phoning the supermarket; nip it in the bud before you sink us."

"I'll refuse to sign any contract with those pigs," he argued.

"Don't be so stubborn, we'll compromise, strike a decent deal. Get us a really good lawyer."

Mr Brown wagged his finger; his wife hadn't ever seen him so irate. "No means no. Principles are principles."

"What do you know about horse racing?"

Thank you Mrs Brown; absolutely sod all. Why couldn't she talk some sense into him?

"How hard can it be? A couple hurdles, back straight, protective barriers and we're as good as gold."

"What about costs, maintenance and licensing?"

"Love, come on tour with me." He took her out back. "Can't you envision 'Mrs Brown's Race Circuit'?"

She fluttered, letting off a quick sigh. "You'd really name it after me?"

Looming grey clouds shadowed the sky. A magpie landed in their unploughed fields; you know the saying, 'one for sorrow'. Unfortunately, nothing could deter his enthusiasm.

"Baby, I'll put your picture on a billboard."

She hugged him, giving him a vote of confidence. And the collapse of sports betting entered step one.

CHAPTER 4

The Great Eight Chase

Mr Brown is the kind of man, once a concept is lodged in his brain, won't let up, like one of those bull terriers with lockjaw. At 6.30 the following morning he drove down to the local council to get planning permission.

"Hey you lot, listen to this."

A crowd of government members surrounded Mr Brown.

"Say it again. You want permission to turn your farm into a what?" asked the man behind a desk.

"To build the best racetrack in the universe," answered Mr Brown.

The laughter could be heard through corridors and walls in adjoining buildings.

"I'm missing the punchline somewhere," said Mr Brown, reclipping his dungarees.

"Never mind. Take these forms, complete them and then send them back, please."

He'd received a one-hundred-and-fifty-page document to apply, always paperwork. After filling out the forms properly, his application would be processed, then approved or rejected. Why didn't they reject it? They could have made up a story about an unsafe environment for horse racing, this whole sorry affair could've been avoided.

After several months, he got the tragic news: his plans had been approved. Boosted beyond words, he attempted to find an investment group to help with the escalating expenses. Everywhere companies in the north asked him the exact same question.

"What the hell do you know about horse racing?"

Now his babbling and muttering may have won over his wife. However, investment companies needed him to sweeten the pot. So on his next scheduled meeting Mr Brown came out all guns blazing. As usual he presented them the slideshow of his farmland and waited for the inevitable question to be put to him.

"Forgive me Mr Brown, what on earth do you know about horse racing? You've run a farm for twelve years. Bit of a jump, no?" said a group member.

"See, once we have opening races this September, we'll make a million pound apiece. My accountant worked out the digits, with tickets and sponsorships. Turnover will be enormous," he smiled.

Mr Brown never had an accountant look over the books. He was getting pretty sick of people telling him what an utterly foolish decision a racetrack was.

The mood in the room was very businesslike; they reviewed his brochure curiously. Two brothers owned the investment company, which bore their name, 'Lame Investments'; they spoke in a sort of code.

"Money is money?"

"Only when it's not money at all."

"Funny money is good money," said the younger, eager brother.

"His money or our money." The older brother was far more reserved.

"His money obviously, our money's safe money," nodded the youngster. Their conversation ended and a deal was struck.

Mr Brown took the two imbeciles to his farm, where they studied the sprawling acres. The ground was mainly uphill and uneven, and a small lake dribbled through the middle of it. The Lame brothers were totally enamoured by cows mooing and sheep baaing.

"Bro, take a pic," the younger immature brother said, grabbing a cow in a headlock.

"Stop clowning about," commanded his brother.

"He's not doing any harm," said Mr Brown.

"Yeah bro, lighten up." He threw Mr Brown the phone.

"On my count, say moo."

"Moo!" he smiled.

The camera phone flash startled the poor cow, who tossed the young man into a fresh pile of cattle dung.

"Looks like Betsy is a bit camera shy," winked Mr Brown.

Young Mr Lame wasn't at all used to country life and reacted hastily, slapping the cow on its nose. Thud! The loud noise resounded off the trees.

"Never slap the cows, whatever you do. That's farm 101," frowned Mr Brown.

"Why? What could possibly happen?"

Both brothers chuckled as the disgruntled cow backed off.

"Yeah, are they gonna spray milk from their udders?" joked the older Mr Lame.

"Semi-skimmed or full fat?" responded young Mr Lame.

The cow didn't wander too far. In fact, she gathered a few friends whilst the two brothers carried on laughing at their stupid wisecracks, quite oblivious.

"What day do cows love?"

"I don't know, what day do cows love?"

"Moooooo-n-day! What else?"

Mr Brown had a strong understanding with his animals, so he gradually withdrew from the field.

Their unwitty remarks kept flowing until powerful hoofs punished the grass. They peeked over their shoulders to see an ungodly sight, a herd of hostile cows stampeding.

Considering the average cow weighs between one thousand four hundred and two thousand five hundred pounds, death by trampling is highly likely. I'd only give you odds of four to one on.

"Get to the gate," ordered Mr Brown.

"Please, I'm seriously sorry, Miss Cow," squealed young Mr Lame.

"I'll pay you to stop, Miss Cow," whined older Mr Lame.

Rich people convince themselves everything can be solved with money. But cows have dignity.

"Run faster, run faster," shouted Mr Brown.

Each brother was ill-equipped for this sudden bout of exercise. Handmade leather shoes and three-quarter-length padded coats restricted their motion to a quick hobble.

Moo! Moo! Moo! The revenge-filled cows hunted in a quest for blood.

"Ditch the jackets, they're weighing you down," instructed Mr Brown.

The men rapidly ripped off their buttons, tossing their coats away. The herd blazed across the field, narrowing the distance. They weren't alone in their pursuit. A dozen or so sheep came to aid their farm friends. Mr Brown waved his business partners frantically forward. With arms going nineteen to the dozen, both Lame brothers slid through the gate. Mr Brown bolted the gate shut.

"Now that's why we never slap cattle. If you want respect, show respect," said Mr Brown.

All three men went into the main farmhouse to get cleaned up.

"This is a three grand suit, I'll bill you for it," moaned Mr Lame.

"No, you won't," admonished his brother.

The two shared a look difficult to describe; it was like one brother had strayed too close to the cliff edge. The young man heeded his warning and dropped it.

"So you can see there's plenty of space to build an extravagant arena."

"Mr Brown, your property shows tremendous potential," praised older Mr Lame, sipping a mug of tea.

"Let's get started. No time like the present."

"Crawl before you can walk, baby steps. We have to sign the deeds." Mr Lame opened his briefcase, placing a legally binding contract on the table.

"Stands bulging with fanatical fans gambling millions, I'm super excited," projected Mr Lame.

Mr Brown, a novice to the world of investments and property development, signed along the dotted line. Extremely unwise. What he'd effectively done was sheer madness. Maximum risk with very low rewards, his contract indicated he'd be at fault for any debt or bad credit. Also, loans would be taken out in his name, and should this establishment turn a profit, Lame Investments would reap its initial money back first.

ALWAYS READ THE SMALL PRINT.

"Now we've got the boring-snoring paperwork completed, let's get creative," toasted old Mr Lame.

To accomplish a goal, sometimes we have to relinquish our cherished possessions. Mr Brown's combine harvester was already on the chopping block. He regrettably sold it below value to raise funds.

None of these men knew anything about designing a racetrack, so outside help was needed. Two weeks later Claudio Rossi, the chief designer of numerous racetracks around Europe, flew in from Milan, first class a must. He arrived at Manchester Airport and was driven straight to the farm, where he'd spend a couple of nights.

A farm in Manchester for Mr Rossi couldn't be further away from the plush apartments of Milan and Rome. The Browns were not used to visitors but welcomed him in. Claudio, shall we say, was quite eccentric. He had long legs for a short man and a tiny but plump upper body like an ostrich.

"Mr Rossi, very nice to meet you," greeted Mr Brown.

Claudio stared at Mr Brown's hand, confused. He knocked his hand away before kissing him on both cheeks.

"OK, this is my wife."

Claudio then gazed at Mrs Brown engagingly; it made her feel uncomfortable.

"Bellissimo, uh," he said.

He hugged her, lifting her off the floor.

"Come on, let me show you to your bedroom," explained Mr Brown, grabbing his luggage.

Mr Rossi whistled and clapped hysterically.

"What's wrong?" asked a scared Mrs Brown.

"Nobody toucha my bag," he spoke with a deep Italian accent.

Mr Brown released the bag so as not to upset Mr Rossi anymore; after all, they were paying him a ton of money to design a racetrack.

"No problem," Mr Brown opened the front door, "this way."

Claudio giggled, planting one hand on his hip and the other out wide in a teapot fashion.

Mr and Mrs Brown were astonished by his strange mannerisms. They didn't know how to take him. He looked friendly yet dangerous, all wrapped up in a silk shirt and skintight leather trousers.

"I have to be at one with my canvas. Feel the soil, taste the air, absorb it into my soul. Bing! Bing! Bing!" Claudio dawdled over to a field, jumping a gate even though it was unlocked.

Sheep watched, baffled.

Mr Rossi pulled out a sleeping bag and bedded in for the night.

"Maybe it's jetlag, love."

"Just lock the door, I don't want him inside the house," said Mrs Brown.

"No arguments from me."

Throughout the night, they heard strange baaing and mooing. However, both husband and wife were too afraid of what they might find to peek.

At 4 a.m., a stiff knock at the window woke them. Mr Brown put on his bathrobe, switching on a small lamp on his bedside dresser. He opened the window with great hesitance to see Claudio hanging on a ledge.

"Mr Rossi, what's going on?" he asked groggily.

"I finish. I go."

"But you've only just got here."

Mr Rossi shoved six pieces of paper into Mr Brown's pocket and slipped off the ledge.

"Don't you need a lift to the airport?" shouted Mr Brown.

"No thanks. I walk, it's quicker."

Claudio Rossi, unsurprisingly, hasn't been seen since. If you meet a middle-aged Italian gentleman roaming the Manchester fields, please avoid him.

The morning following a crazy unbelievable night, the Browns sat down for breakfast.

"I had a strange dream," said Mr Brown.

"Oh yeah?"

"A madman knocked on our window giving me some paper." He dug into his pockets nervously.

As he laid six different pieces of white paper on the table, they saw it was a kind of puzzle. But once arranged in its correct formation, Claudio's talents were clear to see.

"Brilliant, blimey, brass, bold, best, bright, bombastic," boasted Brown.

"He might be a few slices short of a loaf, but his vision is undeniable," cheered Mrs Brown, thinking they were onto a winner.

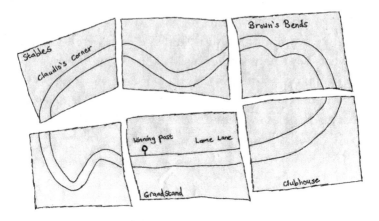

Now we've got the venue sorted, let's meet a couple of participants.

CHAPTER 5

Vintage Red Evens

If there were ever a picture in the dictionary defining a thoroughbred, Vintage Red would sit pretty. The stallion's black coat glowed as it reflected the sunlight. When speaking of dominant athletes, Rafael Nadal, Leo Messi and Lebron James (for NBA fans) may crop up. They're all dwarfed by Vintage Red's overwhelming prowess; he held a record of twenty-nine wins from twenty-nine races.

His owner Mr Philip knew once Vintage was of racing age, he'd tear up the track.

"Treat him like a god, money is always available," said Mr Philip when speaking to trainers.

Owner and horse lived in Marseille, and weren't short a few bob or two. Mr Philip was the second richest man in Europe, worth a reported fifteen billion. He'd inherited the largest vineyard in the world, producing gallons of overpriced wines and champagne. When he received the information of his placing on the rich list, he blew a gasket in fury.

"Second, second place, am I poor?" he cried.

In his stable there were fifty different horses, all thoroughbreds. Vintage always had top billing. He'd be lavished with better equipment, better jockeys. And the stable he slept in was the only one made from red brick instead of wood, with central heating to keep his muscles at optimum temperature. Fresh hay had to be delivered daily as well as endless supplies of water.

Occasionally Mr Philip would enter Vintage Red's stable to chat to him.

"You're my favourite horse, boy. If someone offered me a billion pounds I'd tell 'em to shove off," he said, stroking the stallion's massive body. "Good lad, there, there, that's my boy." He handed his steed a carrot.

Crack! Vintage Red snapped the carrot. To him it was a reward for his excellence.

"You're a gift, a special horse, one in a million." Mr Philip was getting emotional. "Second to None was a fantastic breed, but you're number one."

"Neigh! Neigh," Vintage Red replied.

"'Cause I love you so much, thirty is a nice round number. How about after the next race I retire you from competition?"

Vintage Red didn't mind ending his glamorous career; these brutal training regimes were tiresome.

"I promise you go undefeated and you're done, no more hurdles and steeplechases."

Vintage Red brushed his neck up against his owner joyfully.

The chateau in Marseille was a horse's palace, with multiple staff catering to each specific need.

However, being a priority Vintage Red became the envy of every inferior horse. They hated him rotten. He'd train alone, eat alone. They always imply it's lonely at the top. Vintage Red proved it.

Years before Vintage Red took the mantle of cream of the crop, Second to None won prize money galore. He won the accolade of racehorse of the decade, being lauded as the greatest thoroughbred. So when Vintage Red appeared on the scene as a shy baby foal, Second to None brought him into the winner's circle.

The two were as thick as thieves; Vintage Red absorbed the winner-takes-all mentality. Second to None took his pupil everywhere around the chateau. They'd chat about being separated from their mothers at an early age. Their stables sat opposite each other.

"My mother was a lovely runner, hurdles were her favourite. She flowed with grace and style, very relaxed striding," said Second to None.

"Don't really remember my mum. Soon as I was foaled they took me away and carted me here. I tried to speak to the other horses," replied Vintage Red.

"Never bother son, they'll hate you. Racehorses are a jealous breed, can't stand success."

"But you're friendly, Second to None."

"At some stage in the near future you'll be in my position. Isolated and excluded from their group, when I'm long gone.

31

I'm trying to bridge the gap. Hopefully you'll do the same for your underling."

Vintage Red was growing in height every day, and his neck craned over the barn door. Second to None could see the torment in his eyes. The prospect of another loved one being snatched away pained him.

"Cheer up my man. Number one isn't bad at all. The bonuses can be very fruitful," winked Second to None.

"I don't want to be loathed. Why can't I be normal?" whined Vintage Red.

"You've been given expertise in racing. It's in your blood, son. Don't look a gift horse in the mouth."

They both sniggered.

"How long before my debut?" Vintage Red wondered.

Second to None scouted Vintage Red's bone structure and the sloping of his back.

"You're how old now?"

"Sixteen months," answered Vintage.

"Difficult to say. I started at two, but the way you train, keep improving and it could be as quick as six months."

"I won't be ready in six months for racing." Vintage panicked, stumbling back in his stable.

"Course you will mate. I'll be there to support you."

Through the following days and months, Vintage Red's training regimen was cranked up excessively. More weight would be added to his back. Long runs became longer and hills became steeper.

Then one day Vintage Red and Second to None had their usual race from the embankment that overlooked a French river back to their stables. Second to None always had the best of the young pretender. But now a little more seasoned

Vintage showed that certain *je ne sais quoi* (a quality that cannot be described or named easily).

They both set off from the exact same starting point, a boulder near the river source. Second to None plodded ahead a few lengths. He'd never take it easy on a rookie. He liked him to know who was boss. Flat land was Second to None's speciality; his head bobbed up and down as he flowed home.

"Come on lad, make it challenging," yelled Second to None.

This stirred Vintage Red's competitive edge. Suddenly the black steed flipped a switch, his stride stretched wider and he began gobbling up the ground. Within six or seven strides Vintage Red sneaked in front and that was where the fully grown male would stay.

The resentful horses looked on from their stables, shocked Second to None had been beaten.

"Beginner's luck," said a humble Vintage Red.

"Perfect son, you're one of a kind," glowed Second to None. He was proud a horse like Vintage Red was in line to take his throne.

"But you lost."

"To a better horse, and it is OK. Listen, never be happy with a loss, but accept it and be gracious."

When both superstar horses reached their stables, Mr Philip stood in euphoria.

"My boys, my boys," he gloated.

He waltzed up to Vintage Red, stroking him adoringly. "Time to build your dynasty my friend. A display of that ability is remarkable."

Within six months Vintage Red was entered into the low-key Marseille Classic. A lot of whispers went around about him. Who was he? Why was he so praised? All queries were positively answered with interest. He faultlessly demolished the chasing pack, romping home to victory by half a track.

Another race followed a month later, the outcome being him winning over high hurdles. Newspapers ran with the headlines 'Reinvent-age horse racing' and 'Vintage leaves bookies in the red'.

Mr Philip brazenly worshipped his new whizz kid. And although very green in his career, he threw Vintage's name in the hat for France's biggest race, A Place in Paris. Never before had a race captured the public's imagination in such a way. It was billed as the old versus the new, the young gun against a wise old fox.

Second to None had previously won A Place in Paris on two occasions. No horse had ever won three straight. The thought of another steed beating him over his favoured distance seemed impossible. The contenders all gathered in their stalls waiting for release.

Vintage Red's long face pouted. "Look at this sea of people."

"Get used to it, you're in the big leagues now son," said Second to None.

Both their stalls were next to each other.

"I feel uneasy. My legs are so light."

"That's the pre-race wobbles. They'll disappear, just focus on your stride pattern," instructed Second to None.

"I'm happy you're here with me."

The jockeys were put under starter's orders. Sheer silence gripped the crowd. The gates opened, and what unravelled was impressive. Vintage rushed to first place, controlling his opponents. Second to None chased and chased, hunted and hunted in vain. He got caught in the middle of the pack struggling to find his rhythm; by the time he got into a decent space, Vintage was long gone. Second to None did himself proud in shrinking the deficit but ultimately lost his crown.

That moment was considered, by all, the crowning ceremony of a new legend.

Second to None and Vintage Red never locked horns again. They'd still have conversations in their stables but two months later, Second to None officially retired. Sadly, he left the stables; his area became vacant and Vintage Red's loneliness returned.

He piled up race wins at every prestigious event unchallenged, coasting home in record times.

Mr Philip pledged to retire Vintage after one more outing. And it so happened a personal invite was sent for him to enter the Great Eight Chase.

The Lame brothers acknowledged that his star power would add glamour.

Mr Philip agreed, and an appearance fee of fifty thousand pounds didn't hurt the situation.

A British correspondent flew to France to view Vintage Red and speak to Mr Philip. Vintage Red shimmered. He'd just been pampered, pruned and cleaned.

"What a stunning horse," said the British man.

"Greatest thoroughbred, full stop!" nodded Mr Philip.

"How many more races has he got left?"

"One more and he's out, done. Ain't that right boy," Mr Philip said, patting his muzzle. Vintage preened.

"We've been thinking if he wins in spectacular fashion, he could embark on a world tour, like One Direction. We'll call it a man and his horse," urged the Brit.

Mr Philip paused, caught between honouring a promise to a friend and discovering prominence in a new country.

"I believe with his speed and your unusual mystique, we have a recipe for success."

Vintage raged; he could tell Mr Philip had been swayed.

"Let's talk in my office, shall we?"

CHAPTER 6

Something Good 3/1

As Vintage Red rose to the pinnacle of thoroughbred racing, other horses didn't have it so simple. As Something Good demonstrated, it's not about the horse in the fight, but the fight in the horse. Abandoned by his owner in 2006 outside a train station in St. Petersburg, Russia, Something Good strolled the roads, eating rubbish from dustbins. He slept rough in bus shelters. Under a bridge, young children would throw bricks and stones at his malnourished body. Kids of today, no respect for animals.

Something Good somehow survived the treacherous Russian nights. His drastic weight loss made his ribcage stick out; his overgrown hair gave him little warmth. Something Good's wonderful chestnut coat was caked in filth.

Whilst desperately wandering the city streets, he'd notice big luxurious cars departing the highway. And with whatever energy his body had stored, he dolefully crawled up the motorway, staying on the hard shoulder.

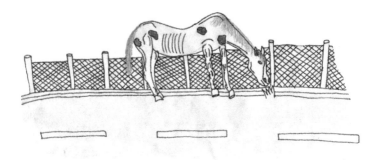

Drivers showered him in abuse.

'Dirty donkey.'

'Why the long face?'

These repeated like chimes in the wind.

Just keep going; don't look back, look only forwards. It's a motto he kept throughout his racing career. Tree leaves were his only source of nutrition, but Something Good's teeth were weak and plastered in plaque, making chewing a terrible chore. The worn down horseshoes clinked along the motorway collecting grit. The experience wasn't pleasant in the slightest; however, through adversity character is created.

For six days straight he dragged himself, catching rainwater on his tongue to stay hydrated. Then finally off the main roads, Something Good saw light at the end of a dreary agony-filled tunnel. He discovered Saints Avenue. Wealth seeped out of this gated community, mansions with helipads, yachts and Rolls Royces for toys.

Famous Russian singers, actors, footballers all neighboured one another. Something Good knew a rich, honourable person would show leniency. Offer him food, refuge and somewhere to bathe.

Unfortunately, the first person to witness the brute was the WAG of a Russian footballing star. As she dropped the top to her convertible Bentley, Something Good barely stood hobbled near an iron gate.

"You putrid beast!" she bellowed in disgust.

Something Good scrambled into an alley, his eyes fogged with tears. He had never displayed any kind of destructive behaviour; all he longed for was a safe home.

The wealthy Russian neighbourhood felt threatened; a vile ragtag animal had interrupted their perfect world. Within hours of his arrival, local authorities were approached to capture the monster.

Numerous animal rescue units were deployed in the area. They scoured the boroughs, bushes and fields. One idiot even rummaged through a sewer. Unlikely hiding place for a six hundred pound horse. Every passing vehicle was searched; vans were stripped down to bare essentials.

The animal rescue team continued dumbfounded before they all gathered for a progress meeting.

"Does anyone think there's no horse?" asked their team leader.

"Rich people are so bored, they waste our time with nonsense," groaned a staff member, placing his dart gun in his boot.

As night drew in, the moon and stars emerged as if they were eager to see the conclusion of this hunt.

"We probably scared him away, poor bugger wasn't gonna get much sympathy around here," the team leader shrugged.

"Best go and collect that hefty cheque," smiled his staff.

"I love gigs without limits. The richer the better I say."

Animal rescue, like all tradesmen, plumbers and mechanics, realise mega-rich people have no concept or value of money. Therefore, a fee of fifteen thousand euros to obtain one horse is deemed plausible. The head of neighbourhood watch made the phone call, so she was responsible for coughing up the pennies.

The chuffed team leader pressed the button to their intercom system. "Excuse me; may I please speak to the lady of the house?"

'Who may I say is calling?'

"Animal rescue and capture."

He waited promptly before the electric gates opened. The Russian woman waited on her porch, unwilling to let common folks into her residence.

"Did you get the awful mongrel?" inquired the woman in a harsh manner.

"He fought and fought, very streetwise. But I'm a professional and satisfaction is guaranteed. How would you like to pay, card, cash or cheque?"

"Where did you find him?"

The man was stumped; luckily lying was part of his job description. He checked his mobile phone for missed calls just to halt proceedings a little. "What we do, love, is spread horseradish on dumpsters, then just play the waiting game."

"Horseradish? You actually expect me to believe that sham of a story?"

"Listen, these horses go mad for it. Why do you think it is called horseradish?" he explained, unclear if she bought it.

"You're the expert," she admitted.

The man breathed a sigh of relief as she began writing out a cheque.

"Now it's customary for clients to tip ten percent on top of our original quotes."

The man had overacted his part in attempting to squeeze out extra money. A great lesson can be learnt here: once you get what you want, don't ask for more!

"Very well, if it's what people do." She threw the cheque away, beginning a fresh one.

"Thank you ma'am. So courteous of you." His heart pumped additional blood to his brain. He judged that if he let wild animals roam wealthy communities, he could charge fortunes to capture them and no-one would be the wiser.

"I'd like to see the horse," commanded the woman.

"Sorry ma'am," he quivered.

"If I'm paying, I'd like to view this beast," she commanded.

"It's messy. Blood, guts, poo. He's in a bad way, put you off your pelmeni," he bartered.

Pelmeni is a traditional Russian dish of dumplings stuffed with minced beef, pork, lamb, fish or mushrooms. Hang on, this isn't a recipe book, I do apologise.

"I've got a cast iron stomach. Now show me the steed," her voice rang with displeasure.

"Or what?" wondered the man.

"My husband's pockets are deep. I'll buy your company and squash it like grapes beneath my feet."

His bottom clenched as he was forced to amble down the drive.

"I warn you, this'll scar you for all your days."

"Behold, you're stalling. One doesn't wait," she said, shoving him away, unlocking the van handle and sliding the shutter up. The steel cage sat unoccupied.

"Where's he gone?" he screamed, pretending to act mystified.

Never tell false information that can haunt you later.

"Teleporting horses, genius technology, what will they come up with next?"

Her eyes drove right into the man's soul as she burnt the cheque before him. "Find it or else, and any more foolish antics, expect serious hell."

The team called for backup. A further two trucks arrived at the scene. Now fifteen animal rescue workers armed with nets, dart guns and night vision goggles stalked Something Good.

"Right, what do we actually know? Facts only please," said the new team leader, quite embarrassed his crew couldn't find a single lonesome animal.

"We're looking for a horse."

"Anything else guys, in four hours. Where's the description. Size, colour? If we don't catch him, there'll be a full inquest."

This announcement lit a fire; some of the unit were already on their second warning; strike three and you're out.

Tension became immense. The moon enriched the sky with sparkle. A spooky silence capped the night. Saint Avenue was cordoned off. Caution tape was stretched around the block. Something Good had the odds firmly stacked against him.

Each team split into different sections, they walked on tiptoes and crept softly.

Something Good got an impression the net might well be tightening. There was a lot of sign language being made between work colleagues. As one sniffed near a statue, weirdly enough of a suspicious-looking chestnut horse, he took a seat. Something Good held the pose for a solid minute.

"When we drove up here there wasn't a figure of a horse," the worker said as he turned to take stock.

Something Good shot off galloping. His pace was hardly blistering, but heart alone gave him an advantage.

A siren resounded and the team went dark, switching off their flashlights; night vision was the order of the day. Something Good's engine ran on fumes, but still he managed to stagger his way into a back alley. Animal rescue cornered him, securing both exits.

"Where you gonna go boy? Can't grow wings, so stop horsing around," chortled a staff member.

Something Good's weakened legs throbbed. He'd never had a simple life and only knew one tactic: fight! The stallion committed everything, all his skin and bones, directly at the two staff members near a seven foot fence. For a weight drained horse, it was a miracle how much momentum he garnered.

"He'll never make it," said a worker as Something Good leaped overhead.

The horse glided over the fence, landing in the back garden of a notable Russian oil tycoon called Mr Vladimir . . . can't pronounce his surname, won't even bother.

Something Good suspected the jig to be up.

Mr Vladimir often enjoyed a glass of vodka after dinner in his garden. So seeing a horse fly over a fence baffled him. Mr Vladimir was a gentleman by nature, a lover, not a fighter. His appearance didn't parade a feeling of kindness. The triangular shaped chin, very broad, but wafer flat nose and transparent blue eyes frightened humans. He wandered down to the collapsed horse, stroking him gently.

"You've been in the wars, haven't you boy."

He took mercy on Something Good, feeding him fruit and storing him in the garage until the morning. Mr Vladimir never had children and treated his horse like a long lost son. During an eight-week period, Something Good amassed tremendous weight and regained his vigour. All the pain he suffered became a memory.

A friend of Mr Vladimir owned stables in Moscow. One glance at a now revived Something Good sent a buzz dancing up his spine.

"That's a mighty fine thoroughbred," he gushed, containing his excitement.

Something Good was shipped off to Moscow to learn the art of racing. He worked his hooves off, motivated by his hard upbringing.

Although his first two races ended up in disappointing losses, the athleticism and promise prevailed. Something Good won sixteen on the trot from there on in; and his defining moment came at the dauntingly named Moscow Winter Classic. Dozens of horses have fallen victim to the sub-zero conditions. Something Good creamed his competitors; he ate up the track, sprinting to victory.

Fame ensued, and a backstory like his made it all the more deserving. When the Great Eight Chase was scheduled, Something Good received his formal invite. On the international race circuit, only Vintage Red held a candle to his supremacy.

Mr Vladimir, a champion in every sense of the word, had been overheard by his loyal steed betting ten thousand euros on Vintage Red to win. They'd stuck together through thick and thin. To know Mr Vladimir fancied another horse finally broke him.

CHAPTER 7

Long Wait 11/2

The Great Chase might be lauded as a two horse race, but don't place a wager just yet. Horses, like humans, over time can change. When you finally think you know someone they'll surprise you in an unexpected way. Long Wait displayed this to a tee.

Most horses, as we are all aware, have big money owners backing them. Sadly for the mares unable to locate a rich parent, they become known as journeymen. They're put into races to fill up the numbers without a prayer of winning.

Long Wait travelled around Japan mostly in a small, portable, uncomfortable stable. Any race available, she'd be carted out, saddle strapped to her back, and a random jockey would mount her to failure. This sequence made her depressed; a total of seventy-one races she'd been involved in during a two-year time frame. Bear in mind the average career of a horse is about forty races.

But what could she do? Can you save a neglected horse? Please donate today at 0800 – just kidding. If Long Wait didn't run an honest race, she wouldn't eat. By her sixth birthday, the mare had clocked up a mind-bending ninety-one races, only placing in four. Her training methods weren't much to shout about; run, stop, run and stop.

Journeymen horses quickly suffer from burnout, as the consistent racing can be wicked on their bodies. Long Wait was a robust horse, very sturdy, her caramel coat showing plenty of meat on the bone. But punters eventually notice the same horse cropping up in multiple races and lose interest, and Long Wait went three months without a race.

"What shall we do with the girl? More trouble than she's worth now," said the head trainer.

"She looks OK though, in decent nick, give her a wash and we'll put her on the open market," replied the stable manager.

They both stared at Long Wait; her stunning caramel glossy blonde tail would have its admirers.

"Once they read her record they'll know she's a dud." The head trainer splashed Long Wait with warm water as her muscles flexed.

"Those thighs are enormous. She has serious horsepower in there."

"It's unlocking it that's the biggest problem," said the trainer.

"Fantastic! We'll put on a claiming race, shoving all our no hopers in a melting pot. Long Wait will walk it. And we'll cash in."

The men high fived. Their plan would comprise anything with four legs and a heartbeat. Horses were set to race a one-mile straight in Tokyo. Only a handful of spectators observed, but Long Wait understood all it takes is one person to believe in you.

The horses, to say the least, weren't in fabulous shape. Bulging stomachs, wobbly neck fat, chipped hoofs and missing teeth were a few examples. As predicted, Long Wait edged it by a nose hair from the stands; if you squinted super hard, she resembled a half-good thoroughbred.

A Japanese-based technology group saw a glimmer of ambition in her. They say you can tell a real thoroughbred through a desire in their eyes.

Claiming races go on behind closed doors. Unwanted horses are put up for auction, win, lose or draw. Because Long Wait won, she became the main attraction. Excitedly she neighed, spinning her ravishing blonde hair when trotted onto centre stage. The room was barely lit; a powerful beam smartly hidden under the stage bloomed, and her gold jacket twinkled like a thousand flawless diamonds.

The auctioneer had the gift of selling down pat. As the platform Long Wait stood on rotated, the bidding began.

"Here we have a notoriously unique mare; her delightfully dazzling golden coat conceals a stupendous animal. Ready to make you a boatload of cash, now let's start at one hundred thousand yen."

The woman in the corner held up her card, bidding; she liked Long Wait for her daughter.

"One hundred thousand to the woman in the skirt, do I hear two hundred thousand?" asked the auctioneer.

The Japanese group raised to two hundred thousand yen swiftly.

"Right, two hundred thousand yen from the peculiar gentlemen on table two." I'd never recommend insulting your customers, but everyone has their own quirky style.

"Five hundred thousand yen," yelled the woman, glaring at the men.

"Hey big spender, these poor souls can't compete."

I get it, the auctioneer was a bully. He'd back bidders into a corner, forcing them way over budget.

"Well. For five hundred thousand yen going once," said the auctioneer with a sort of arrogance.

The Japanese men calculated their funds.

"Our professor needs a stern horse to be his guinea pig," one guy whispered.

"Yeah, but five hundred plus is steep. If his theory doesn't work we'll be broke."

"Going twice," shouted the auctioneer, grabbing his gavel.

The lady screeched in passion.

Her squeal echoed down the men's eardrums. Each guy sweated as they glanced up at Long Wait on stage, who flicked her tail in a ladylike manner.

"One million yen," bellowed the men nervously.

The auctioneer froze, confused. "A million yen for this horse. OK, going once."

Quietness patrolled the auction house. Most people kept schtum in fear of mistakenly bidding.

"Going twice and sold to the crazy gentleman on table two." His gavel struck the sounding block and Long Wait was bought.

For your curiosity, one million yen converts to about five thousand nine hundred pounds. I'm a Japanese millionaire people.

Long Wait may have had delusions of a proper owner spoiling her with presents in abundance, but it couldn't have been further from the truth.

High Spec Techs were a group of Japanese scientists. They would often have vicious arguments over whether it was possible to take a mediocre horse to championship level with technology.

The mare faced daily testing and analysis. They checked her body fat percentage and conformation.

After stern examination results found her obese, a crash course diet was identified.

"Old girl's put on a bit of timber," explained a professor.

"Should change her name to heavyweight," replied a student.

The room exploded in giggles.

She loathed comments on her weight, as all women do. However, her hooves were tied. Whatever the professors whipped up, she'd gobble down. Portion sizes were massively reduced to shrink her stomach, and her protein intake was doubled. The protein made her muscles recover faster, giving her more stamina. Calcium vitamins were also introduced to strengthen her bones.

Long Wait wasn't looked at as a horse anymore. She had been referred to as subject one, hooked up to a variety of computers and gadgets. A specially made treadmill was installed with each function representing different terrains and conditions. Sensors monitored her hoof pressure.

"She seems to favour her left side," announced a student reading the screen.

"We need balance, that's where she's losing speed."

The professor set about building ultra-lightweight aluminium horseshoes capable of easing her left-sided favouritism.

When she originally entered the lab her average time for a mile stood at a ghastly two minutes twenty-six seconds. After a few tweaks, her average trickled down to a snappy one minute thirty-five seconds, definitely thoroughbred territory.

"Experiment proved successful," boasted the professor to his class.

"Don't we have to race her to see how she fares against opposition?"

So it went. Long Wait's new streamlined physique would be unleashed onto the Tokyo crowd. In total, the mare had lost forty-five kilos and looked fabulous, might I add. The blonde locks had been plaited in a crisscross. Long Wait caused casual fans to pack arenas. Tiny jockeys fought for the right to ride her.

The pretty girl, as commentators described her, blazed the Japanese racetrack. And with only five races under her newly tighter-fitting belt, she booked her ticket to the Great Eight Chase.

"See, who's the man? Got our money back and then some," crowed the professor.

"Can she win the Chase?" asked his students.

The professor gazed at his golden girl, her renaissance remarkable and superb. He gauged Vintage Red or Something Good would have her beat.

"I'd be happy with third place," conceded the professor, quite upbeat.

"So why bother if she couldn't win?"

The professor grinned; all along, he had a long game plan. "If I can get this girl to make babies with a stud like Vintage Red, think of the possibilities!" His eyes glazed over, awash in dollars, yen, pounds, euros and any other currency. "The prodigy child, the chosen one, angel kid. He'd be magnificent."

Long Wait didn't want kids; she'd only just begun feeling good about herself. A child would spell the end to her racing career.

CHAPTER 8

Advertising and Marketing

Having officially signed a trio of stellar thoroughbreds, the Lame brothers searched for some sponsorship deals. Advertising was where they'd recoup a lot of their investments. To make a statement about their marketability, the owners of Vintage Red, Something Good and Long Wait were all invited over from their native homelands.

Mr Philip and Mr Vladimir shared a bit of needle. The two billionaires squabbled like children.

"Mr Vladimir, you look well," said Mr Philip.

"I had a glorious sleep on my private jet," bragged Mr Vladimir, wise to the fact Mr Philip had recently sold his own jet. Oh, the poverty. I know I feel sorry for him. Not.

"I'm awaiting my new jet, it's on order," replied Mr Philip.

"New jet? I heard nothing of this."

"Only elite customers. Maybe you could join their waiting list," said Mr Philip, handing him his business card.

"You'll be able to call anytime. For discounts, just say Mr Philip is a close personal friend."

Ding, ding. Round one to the Frenchman.

Tick-Tock Clocks was the first company to lend its name to the event. Not without a few hoops to jump through, though.

The Lame brothers, Mr Brown and the three horse owners waited in a conference room for a Tick-Tock representative.

While waiting, the professor decided to pester Mr Philip on Vintage Red. "Your horse, how tall is he?"

"A towering twenty hands high," said Mr Philip.

"Something Good stands at an all-conquering twenty point five hands," blasted Mr Vladimir, taking round two.

Mr Vladimir understood aggravating Mr Philip would duly impact Vintage Red's performance, making his bet safe.

The Lame brothers saw this and loved that their two biggest names fought like cat and dog.

"My horse has won twenty-nine on the trot, he's unbeaten, a freak of nature," gloated Mr Philip.

"Your boy has never been up against a specimen like Something Good. Not even Second to None could rival my lad's intensity."

Mr Philip seethed. Speaking of previous horses was a low blow. "Never mention his name."

"Why? Face facts, your horses aren't tough. Weak, just like their owner. Cherrypicked opponents, stuffed records. Unlike Something Good, he had a terrible road to glory."

"Padded records? Well we'll see in two months. Tell your stallion to bring his A game and get used to seeing Vintage Red's backside."

Round three to Mr Philip. Only just.

"Would you say your horse's back legs are normal size for a thoroughbred?" asked the professor.

"Everything is in equal proportion," replied Mr Philip, unnerved by these probing questions.

"Would you describe his eyes as stable and clear?"

The professor had rattled Mr Philip, who switched seats with Mr Brown, fearing for him and his horse's safety.

"Why are you so interested in my horse?" pondered Mr Philip.

"Just scouting the competition is all, want to know it's an even playing field." The professor had a massive tell when lying. He'd scratch his right palm. He scratched frantically.

"You OK mate?" asked Mr Brown.

"A slight rash. Not used to the British climate."

"The winner of the Great Eight Chase will be the best horse. No underhand tactics will be accepted. Failure to comply with rules and regulations means automatic disqualification and a one million pound fine," explained young Mr Lame.

Mr Vladimir and Mr Philip chuckled.

"One million, that's pocket money," bragged Mr Vladimir.

"I tip waiters at restaurants more, pay my maids and butlers more. Even the gardener and window cleaner get bigger bonuses," proclaimed Mr Philip.

Mr Vladimir didn't like this game of one-upmanship. "Always trying to top me, aren't you?"

"Heavens, what are you speaking of?"

"I buy a plane. You buy a plane. I buy an island. You buy an island. I buy a football team. You buy a football team," ranted Mr Vladimir.

"I'm better looking than you. Stronger, faster and richer – how on God's green earth am I trying to top you?"

Mr Vladimir zipped it for the remainder of the meeting. And the winner by fourth round knockout; hailing from Marseille, France, Mr Philip.

"Does Vintage Red have any aggression or problems with mares?"

"Professor, I will no longer answer questions on my horse," groaned Mr Philip.

The Lame brothers became giddier.

"Those two should have a TV show," whispered young Mr Lame.

By this time, Mr Philip and Mr Vladimir were arm wrestling for ten million pounds (yesterday's interest for them).

"Yes they should, it'll be enthralling, all eight horse owners around a table. We'll call it the great eight debate," responded old Mr Lame.

They'd been waiting all of twenty minutes before a Tick-Tock rep arrived.

"Gentlemen, sorry for the delays," said the representative, looking a bit perturbed at the two billionaires arm wrestling in the corner.

"Sorry won't cut it. We've got several meetings with major sponsors that'll have to be rearranged," announced old Mr Lame.

"I can only offer my deepest apologies," he humbly stated.

The Lame brothers' eyes twinkled in the representative's direction. He was about to receive a lesson in business from a bunch of specialists. The brothers abruptly stopped the battle of the billionaires, which was heading for a stalemate anyway. They were either incredibly strong or pathetically weak.

"We'll have to speed through the business aspect, just get down to facts and figures," said young Mr Lame.

"Now don't play games. Time.co and Big Hand Little Hand clocks have already set the bar pretty high," added old Mr Lame.

The representative panicked, rubbing his forehead strenuously as if someone had stuck a sticker on it. He revised his offer, jotting down a new deal. A glamorous event like the Chase would boost a company's profile.

"I think you'll agree we've been extremely favourable." He slid a cheque across the table.

The men were jumping out their seats; a seven-figure sponsorship deal scrambled their business brains. Most of them were ready to snap off Tick-Tock's arm and accept terms. All but two men weren't so won over. Mr Philip and Mr Vladimir had a little conflab off to one side. They returned to the table with a verdict.

"Your sponsorship deal meets our requirements. However, Time.co offered us complementary gold watches," said Mr Vladimir.

"Custom made with specific engraving if preferred," chimed in Mr Philip.

One thing I've always known about billionaires: as rich as they are, free still gets their pulses racing.

And the rich get richer. Against his better nature, the representative accepted their proposal.

Each man left Tick-Tock with gold watches. Bling! Bling!

They replayed this routine at a gadget company, walking away with new computers, as well as a lifetime's supply of soft drinks and a year's worth of new shoes and clothes from a retail outlet. What a difference a day makes.

CHAPTER 9

Heartbreaker 8/1

You didn't think there could be an extravagant championship without an American contender? He might not have been a conventional horse, but Heartbreaker was as American as peanut butter and jelly sandwiches. The stud wore an alluring bay-coloured coat, which appeared glossy like melted milk chocolate.

Heartbreaker grew up on a ranch in Austin, Texas with traditional cowboys. He wasn't the first horse to have this existence and wouldn't be the last. In fact, a handful of horses lived on the ranch; saying they had it cushy is putting it lightly. Cowboys protected them like babies, with regular meals, grooming and sublime views of bumpy mountains and hills being highlighted in the baking sunshine. Each steed only worked in three-month rotations, meaning three months on, three months off, so they got six months' downtime out of the year.

"This is heavenly," said a female horse. "Living any other way would be sinful."

She and Heartbreaker had taken a trip down to the lake for a refreshing sip of water. The water was navy blue and would roll up the rocks. There was a crack in the belly of a mountain where the water tasted super sweet, not poisoned with too much salt.

"Delicious, really energising," she said. "Are you not thirsty, Heartbreaker?"

"No, I'm OK thanks."

"What's the matter with you?"

"Nothing," said Heartbreaker, wandering away from the mountain.

"Come and tell me. I'm your friend," she bugged him.

Heartbreaker stood near the lake and stared at his reflection in the sunlit liquid. "It's tedious and dull, what are we achieving here?"

"We round up cows, and all your friends are here that love you."

Heartbreaker shrugged, galloping back to the ranch.

His female companion rushed to keep up. "Slow down, Speedy Gonzales. Some of us are running on a full fuel tank."

The Great Eight Chase

Over the next few weeks, Heartbreaker became more reclusive. The fed up steed developed into an antisocial animal. He wouldn't talk or eat for days.

"You have a word with him," whispered the horses to his only lasting friend.

Heartbreaker's silence had sent him barmy. The stallion barked instead of neighing. And he would hop the gates, wandering into the road barking at baffled drivers and passers-by. On Sundays, Heartbreaker could be seen climbing trees.

He also decided to only walk on his hind legs.

His unusual larking about wasn't going unnoticed by the ranch cowboys. Eventually, they discussed the situation of their irritating animal.

"Shall we sell him?" said cowboy one.

"He's a good boy just playing up," said cowboy two, watching Heartbreaker spit into the air and try to catch it back in his mouth.

Don't act innocent. Like you haven't experimented. Oh, you haven't? No, me neither, that'd be disgusting.

"Look, he's become a liability and a danger to the other horses," said cowboy one.

"Just needs a little coaching and adjusting, channel his energy in the right direction," replied cowboy 2.

"He's a kooky, mad, crazy, off his nut mate. Not even the four horsemen could stabilise him."

Cowboy two frowned. "Four horsemen?"

"Yeah, the four horsemen, they're horses that look like men."

Cowboy two sighed. "There's a movie called *The Four Horsemen*. But please don't tell me you actually thought four horses were wearing suits roaming the planet?"

"Don't be dumb, how gullible do I seem?" replied a redder than red cowboy one.

Heartbreaker was excluded from regular ranch activity, being put through a series of sporting events to see which fit him best. The horse's adventurous nature made him welcome new challenges with open hooves. They pursued a career in polo, where rich men sit on steeds chasing a ball with a stick. After two sessions Heartbreaker came to the conclusion polo was an utterly useless sport played by lazy men.

Equestrianism, commonly known as show jumping, sees participant and horse run round a circuit jumping hurdles. Penalties are incurred by touching obstacles, knocking down barriers and failing to jump. Sounds riveting to me; alas Heartbreaker tired of the trotting about in circles, although he loved launching himself over the hurdles. He'd clear hurdles three or four times for fun, not even looking remotely like clipping a barrier.

Cowboy two saw his bravery over bigger obstacles.

A gentleman sitting two rows behind gaped at the horse, hoisting himself out of his seat. "The boy would make a terrific hurdler, he's in the wrong field," he said.

The Great Eight Chase

A lot of things in a horse's life happen by chance. An unsuspecting individual might blurt something out at random. His words find the right targets and a new star is born.

Cowboy two that night purchased a book called *How to Turn a Horse into a Winning Thoroughbred in Weeks*. Bit of a longwinded title, granted. According to cowboy two, it was the greatest six dollars ninety-nine cents ever spent. Tendon boots were bought; blinkers were attached to keep Heartbreaker focused on the track. And three weeks after being registered, Heartbreaker took his initial dip in the thoroughbred racing waters. It wasn't a festival of A1 horses; most of the contestants edged nearer to the end of their careers than the beginning.

Heartbreaker broke away in earnest, striding ahead, clobbering the sand track, his flair flourishing and his excitement swelling. He couldn't contain himself. Pro trainers call it running the race early, where an eager horse rushes off unproductively. Heartbreaker, despite being a free spirit, still suffered from nerves and decelerated, resulting in finishing third place.

"All those bucks spent on trailers, trainers and reading a book? Look at the egg on your face," said cowboy one.

"You'd have me submit when he was leading for ninety percent of the race. Fat chance anyway, he's built for hurdles, not flat racing."

Heartbreaker arrived home, motivated by a third. His happiness radiated in practice. He'd finally learned to take orders and advice from others, which we all should do. He halted his barking; climbing trees didn't float his boat either. The leaner, cleaner and more disciplined steed approached life with a new perspective. He became a model horse around the ranch.

"What's gotten into you?" his lady friend asked.

"This beautiful country of ours, I'm a city boy. No more outback simpleton living. I'm gonna become America's very best racehorse," he cheered, kicking his front legs into the air.

His lady friend smiled to see her buddy focused and exuberant. It reassured her he wouldn't be put down.

"Do it for the steeds on the ranch that always adored you."

They wandered to the lake one very last time, as Heartbreaker readied to depart for mission USA.

Heartbreaker set out to accomplish racing immortality. Las Vegas, New York and Los Angeles were stomping grounds of his. In a three-year run, Heartbreaker won nine out of twenty-seven pro races. A win percentage of thirty-three percent; arithmetic keeps the brain effective. His stats wouldn't jump off the page at you.

Well, if he wasn't that fast, how could he compete in the Great Eight Chase?

Thank you for asking! So you are engaged.

Heartbreaker didn't obtain his name because of his tall, dark and striking frame. Actually his real name was Paul; not very spectacular. Sorry to any Pauls reading this.

Although his racing record remained stagnant, he had a distinct habit of winning the big ones. Place him in a race with seven rocking horses and watch him straggle. Give him seven elite stallions and mares, see him smoke their hooves.

Heartbreaker's path wasn't guaranteed like Vintage Red, Something Good or Long Wait. He had to qualify for the Chase in an all-star cast in New Jersey. He relished the atmosphere, absorbing the ocean of viewers. He thought to himself that whatever happened, he was a winner to go from a ranch to this ultimate contest. While Heartbreaker was frozen in deep thought, the tape was drawn back, and all other horses sped off.

"Our boy's got some work to do," said cowboy one.

"Our boy?" fumed cowboy two.

"Yes, don't be so surprised. We co-own the ranch. He's from our stables."

As the race came into its final stages Heartbreaker's supercharged thighs tensed, demanding more from his hooves. They responded immediately. And so would go Heartbreaker's passage to Manchester. I wouldn't have bet against him.

CHAPTER 10

Nothing More 11/1

Now people have a lot of opinions about Germany, and they don't always paint it in the most glowing of lights. The thing with opinions is they can never be facts. Regrettably, Nothing More doesn't play her part in dispelling the rumour.

She thrived and thrived in Hamburg. She won and stun; roasted and boasted in Germany. I'm trying to be elaborate, bulking out her chapter.

Can you tell?

Because the truth remains, Nothing More did exactly as her title suggests. The most significant item she owned was her brown and white spotty coat. Around the paddock, her nickname was the Dalmatian horse. Boy, I'm struggling. She had a long neck. I mean really long. Other horses hated living next door because on occasion her extended neck would arch over and steal their hay.

The girl never seemed particularly fond of racing. On tracks, stallions and mares bask with elation; the thrill of a chase puts a delightful sheen in the eyes of proper thoroughbreds. Nothing More gave it her all out there. No one was questioning her abilities. Only after every single win, something seemed missing; she'd wander off the track back to her stable.

But then again her owner wasn't dripping in flair and zeal. Mrs Griffiths had owned Nothing More since her foaling in 2012, and they had a strictly efficient relationship. There was no late night bareback riding in the scintillating moonlight. Weekly Mrs Griffiths looked over the running costs, collecting receipts for her mare.

"Is she still in peak condition?" she asked coaches.

"Yes ma'am, I expect in the next couple of years you'll see her in her prime."

"Good. Maybe then I'll profit."

"Her balance is incredible, and how she keeps speed while jumping is legendary," gushed the coach.

"As she should be. I don't pay you to make her average. Do I?" said Mrs Griffiths.

"She's fast and lean like her owner," grovelled the coach. He showed her a video on an electronic device in slow motion, zooming in to concentrate on Nothing More's formidable balance.

"What am I looking at precisely?"

"Her landing. She's able to switch weight from back to front. Rare, rare dexterity."

Mrs Griffiths rejected his spouting about shifting weight. The woman was infamously hard to please. She had made her fortune in paint. Not paintings; her family are the biggest paint suppliers in the world. I'm practically positive at least one of your walls is splashed with Griffiths' paint, 'decorating places since people had faces'.

Nothing More had the tag of darling of the track; punters love a safe bet. Mrs Griffiths got a magazine article written about her. 'More Behind the Owner' was a prudent and innovative headline, shame the news reporter wrestled to get answers from Mrs Griffiths. If you think getting blood from a stone is difficult, you should attempt an interview with this lady. I'll give you a few examples of how not to conduct yourself in an interview.

After all, I haven't got anything better to do.

Never leave the reporter waiting. And if you're running late, phone first, apologise, give them an excuse, you were abducted by aliens or infected by zombies. Rescuing orphans from burning buildings can't lose. Secondly, dress to impress: clean, classy and conservative. Mrs Griffiths' dress sense was as uncomplicated as making ice. She wore a black skirt and white shirt Monday to Sunday, sometimes with a cardigan or blouse. Be happy, warm; make it feel like it's a friendship not an obligation.

"Welcome, Mrs Griffiths," smiled the reporter.

"Let's get this done already," snapped Mrs Griffiths.

The reporter lady hit 'record'. She wasn't used to such bluntness.

"Being a woman horse owner, do you feel you're treated differently?"

"No. Next question."

"They say a racehorse is the most expensive pet; do you believe that's an accurate statement?"

"Yes," answered Mrs Griffiths, repeatedly looking at the clock.

"Care to give me an idea of the daily routine of a horse owner?" asked the reporter, somehow maintaining her politeness.

"You buy food, they eat, give them stables and they stay. Give them tracks and they run."

"It must be heartening seeing your steed cross the line first."

"Sure."

See what I mean? Drawing blood from a cold, angry and old stone chewing cement would be easier. Nevertheless, the reporter persisted but the answers became shorter and more abrupt. A nod or shake represented yes or no after a while. Annoyed, the reporter scrapped the article, stating, I quote, "This woman is rude, obnoxious and doesn't deserve to be remembered or written about, full stop." See? Bad behaviour gets you nowhere.

"Thank you for taking time out of your busy schedule, Mrs Griffiths."

"Whatever," Mrs Griffiths huffed, storming out of the room.

Nothing More isn't to blame for her lack of spark; her owner is. You can't expect a pet to grow up happy in an unhappy environment. She knew her position as well. Win more than you lose. The coaches tried encouraging the girl to display extra mastery in events. Act like she belonged, sashay

69

instead of walking, be confident, embrace her long neck. Jockeys stroked her and patted her spotted coat. Nothing More plainly plodded back to her stables.

She feared the day when her legs wouldn't carry her across the finishing line. Luckily, at only three years Nothing More could run for years to come. Out of all the horses I've mentioned she actually had a better winning streak; no one on this list can boast six wins in four weeks. But she can. To add to her CV, only two animals in the Chase were undefeated: Vintage Red and herself.

In Hamburg, a street was going to be named after her until Mrs Griffiths made a few ungodly remarks to the local mayor. Still, on the racetrack business continued as normal and championships accumulated. And with hype now galvanised, Mrs Griffiths anticipated Nothing More's seat at the Great Eight Chase was practically certified.

Day upon day she'd check email, phone, texts, Skype, even fax machine.

Fax machine?

A telephonic transmission; basically it scans paper to another fax machine using telephone numbers. I'm bored already. Look at it like sending an email from a Mac, just not as good.

Whispers spread that Nothing More would be shunned because of an irritating owner. Whispers always end up in the wrong earholes, why is that? Mr Griffiths, the long-suffering husband, knew his wife inside out. She'd stomp, storm, grunt and groan day and night.

"They still haven't phoned. My horse has a perfect record. Why haven't they called?" whined Mrs Griffiths, her face flushed.

"Listen you'll blow your top being all livid, relax."

She kept restarting her computer, checking her wireless connection signal.

"How can they snub me? How do those pesky idiots think this'll bother me? I won't be riled. Without Nothing More, their whole event loses respectability. Help me understand how the finest female thoroughbred isn't automatically entered! Numbers never lie and this girl's the truth."

Mr Griffiths watched her bounce off the walls, doors and ceilings.

"Why? Why? Why?" she'd shout.

It became so aggravating that Mr Griffiths went to work early at 5 a.m., arriving back for 8 p.m. He'd take scenic routes for substantial peace and harmony; a murky night sky laced with stardust alleviated his tension. He yearned for the Great Eight Chase to commence so this sorry chapter of their life could be terminated.

He parked up on the drive making sure he didn't block Mrs Griffiths' Audi. It was a sin he committed once and just managed to live to tell the tale.

When he opened the front door, an invigorating aroma of *eintopf* (German stew) hit him for six.

"There he is, my wonderful hubby," said Mrs Griffiths, almost cracking a smile.

"What information am I missing here?" asked a bewildered Mr Griffiths.

"Follow me, sweetheart." This time there was a definite smile.

A framed invitation sat on the dining room table. It specifically summoned Nothing More to a qualifying competition in Berlin.

"She's in like Flynn." Mrs Griffiths hugged her husband for the second time in their four-year marriage.

Nothing More glided to race win thirteen in Baden Baden. Next stop, Manchester. Her owner barrelled down the stand to see her.

"Move out my way. Where is she?" ranted Mrs Griffiths.

Nothing More had predictably ambled back to her stables.

"That's my girl, that's my gorgeous mare." Mrs Griffiths oozed praise on the horse, kissing her muzzle. "You made mummy so happy today darling."

The mare had finally gained recognition for her fantastic exploits. Self-assured, confident, she bristled in training. Positivity rekindled her spirit. Her speed had vastly improved too. A tireless work ethic is a valuable commodity. Good books don't just write themselves. Nothing More outworked all horses known to man, grinding for perfection.

Deep tissue massages were required twice a week. Seeing the adoring glint in Mrs Griffiths' eyes propelled her to exert further force. Nothing More thrust and thudded recklessly, ignoring her pain barrier.

After an energy-depleting routine, Nothing More went for a final jump. The fence wasn't particularly high. She wearily plodded up, and with a certain grace the front legs cleared; unfortunately her back legs didn't fare so well. She grazed the hedge, losing symmetry, landing awkwardly on her front hooves.

"NEIGH!" she howled.

A top-ranked German vet examined the hurt mare. Mr and Mrs Griffiths stared on in silence with bated breath. Nothing More had an X-ray and blood sample taken. She rested for forty-eight hours, waiting for the verdict.

A deeply sombre mood drowned the house of Griffiths in pity. Nothing More seemed rickety and hesitant. The German vet hauntingly crept up the footpath; his black over-coat made him appear like the grim reaper.

"Mr Griffiths," he said in reverent tones.

"She's my horse, address me," piped Mrs Griffiths.

"It is bad news I'm afraid. Your horse suffered a rupture of the superficial digital flexor tendon."

"What? Speak human man, not vet mumbo jumbo."

The vet dumbed it down for them. "A tendon joins muscle to bone, it's a support beam. A rupture this severe takes on average ten to fifteen months to repair. And they're never the same from there on in."

"She has a race in two months. What can we do?" cried Mrs Griffiths.

The vet gently placed his hand on her shoulder. "Pray to the heavens for a miracle. There's nothing more modern medicine can do."

The Griffiths walked over to the stable, peering at the damaged leg. The mare, disappointed and downcast, flopped on the hay.

"Unfortunate girl. The Chase gave her vitality," said Mr Griffiths, tearing up.

"And still will."

"You heard him. It'll take a year for her to be ready."

"My girl's running no matter what," declared Mrs Griffiths.

Nothing More's leg throbbed in excruciating soreness. In her heart of hearts, she feared the Great Eight Chase would be her ultimate resting place.

CHAPTER 11

Television Bidding

As it so happened, this shambles of a race featured three awesome thoroughbreds and two excellently talented animals in supporting roles. Seemed the three musketeers (Young, Old Mr Lame and Mr Brown) could do no wrong. They felt bulletproof, like they could walk on water. Take a shower without getting wet. At present the three bozos were listening to a TV network's proposal. A terrestrial channel would be ideal for a nationwide audience.

"We judge our station is a perfect fit," said the network manager.

"I hear a lot of talk, I like facts and figures, numbers. Reveal your intentions."

The Channel 74 executive prepared a slideshow and pie chart. The lights were dimmed and a mellow jazzy music hummed through a speaker. The trio couldn't thwart an urge to loosen their goose. Each gentleman slouched, taking off their ties, absorbing the marvellous technicalities.

"We have a market share of sixty-five percent, the largest among any network, including several sports stations," added the executive.

"Meaning what?" The business jargon mostly went over Mr Brown's head. He'd usually sit and observe. You can take the man out of the farm, but not the farm out of the man.

"Essentially six point five out of ten people are glued to my station," he informed them.

Mr Brown was not a maths whizz by any stretch.

"How can there be half people?" he asked.

"It's worked out on average. Say ten million are viewing television."

Mr Brown nodded, trying to keep track. "Ten million, I'm with you."

"Well, six point five million of those people will be watching us."

"That's a lot of people," confirmed Mr Brown.

"Honestly, we'll offer you full press coverage, billboards and free promotion. No other networks approach our dedication," he said.

Mr Brown welled up with glee and launched across the table. "Think you make a sound argument. Hopefully this'll be a groundbreaking partnership."

"Now we don't want to give you the impression you're not a leading candidate. However, other steeds race too," said Old Mr Lame, throwing ice on the fire.

"But you lot, my pockets are bare," panicked Mr Brown. Nutty Claudio Rossi's stadium design had swallowed up more money than forecast.

The Lame brothers conferred. They'd learnt some subtle business traits from Mr Philip and Mr Vladimir, who were embroiled in a war trying to buy a guitar signed by

Jimi Hendrix; sixty-two million euros was the most recent number touted around.

"How should we conduct ourselves?" wondered young Mr Lame.

"Aggressive. Play hardball. Don't let your guard down," replied his more sensible brother.

"Good lord, we might pull this off," speculated young Mr Lame.

"Should I draw up the legal paperwork?" asked the executive.

Mr Brown, so intent on having television backing, brought his own pen. The plastic biro was unable to halt his enthusiasm, snapping and splurging black ink across the Golden Oak oval table.

"Somebody's bursting to lay down some ink," the exec joked, calling for a cleaner.

"How's about it then? We bang out a deal, I'll take you out for a spot of lunch afterwards."

"Hold your horses. We're not saying neigh, but we need to feel stable," quipped Old Mr Lame.

"You do know Channel 74 is the biggest operating station? We have the most appeal to a mass audience, strictly speaking. Cash no one can equal."

A number in the mid-six-figure region piqued the Lame brothers' curiosity.

Mr Brown quietly stewed in the stress-filled office. Were the Lame brothers trying to bite the hand that was making generous efforts to feed them?

"Steedy on fella, everyone's jockeying for position," said young Mr Lame, winking.

"To get the promotion ball rolling, I'll need an answer pronto." The exec's voice squeaked slightly, a hint of weakness perhaps.

"There's a lot to ponder. We'll get back to you shortly," said old Mr Lame, shaking the executive's hand.

As the three men began exiting the room, a strange tingling crept up old Mr Lame's forearm. In a complete act of absurdity, the executive went off the cuff, not following company policy.

"One million guaranteed upfront."

Mr Brown's head exploded, not literally. "A mil! Did he say a million?"

The Lame brothers jumped for joy inside. Externally, though, they were composed, like one million pounds to own the broadcasting rights was a mere drop in the ocean.

"Definitely food for thought. However, we're seeking longevity," stated old Mr Lame.

"A million a year for an initial three years," begged the executive.

"Tempting. Give us until the end of the day." Old Mr Lame had Channel 74 eating out of the palm of his moisturised hand.

Mr Brown stormed into the lift. "You two nitwits, where's your brains?"

"Nitwits, farm boy? Knew we should have left him home, shearing pigs," replied young Mr Lame.

"You shear sheep, moron."

"Moron. What's with the name calling?" said old Mr Lame.

The lift shuffled down a few floors to their next meeting on floor fifty-four.

"If you don't like or understand business then walk away, farm boy."

Mr Brown indignantly flared his teeth and clamped his bottom lip. Old Mr Lame wished this lift would reach its destination rapidly.

"Getting mad, farm boy? Come on then. I'll have you know I've watched every Jackie Chan and Bruce Lee movie numerous times."

(Hardly makes him a kung fu wizard).

"OK crouching tiger, let's go." Mr Brown, infuriated, ripped shirt buttons off.

They squared up, going forehead to forehead, growling.

Before a punch landed, the lift doors slid apart.

Employees of Channel 54 stared horrified at two hooligans brawling in a lift.

"You're causing a scene, smarten up," admonished old Mr Lame.

Mr Brown's anger tapered off. He buttoned up his blazer, regaining poise.

If the gentlemen expected the royal treatment, they were terribly mistaken. Channel 54 was widely considered bottom of the barrel in telly land. Their offices were only six by six foot cubicles. The clattering of fingertips hitting keyboards could be heard and seen. Desks were made from cheap material. A potent breeze could've collapsed their workstations. Typewriters replaced computers. The only use of the internet was a single laptop; queues ran up to six hours.

"Let's just go back to Channel 74 with our tail between our legs," said Mr Brown.

"Never judge a book by its cover my friend, the words inside define the true importance," replied old Mr Lame.

You only get one chance to make a first impression, and Channel 54 failed. A meaty-looking man came waddling over, his mammoth third chin burying his neck. Every couple of metres he'd pause and sit down, frazzled.

"We'll come to you," said young Mr Lame, saving the man from going into cardiac arrest.

"Think it's for the best, don't stride like the twenty stones of fury I used to be," he said, gasping for air.

The men stepped into a quieter, isolated office. Fast food brochures were piled on his desk.

"Sorry about the sitting arrangements. Times are hard."

Mr Brown and the Lame brothers sat on plastic crates, repulsed.

"I'd offer you a drink see, but taps in the toilets are broken, so thirst it is," he explained.

"We're plenty hydrated thanks, let's crunch some numbers," said Mr Brown.

The Channel 54 boss scrambled through sheets of paper. No slideshow or bewitching music were included. "Ah, we propose for every five million viewers you'll receive fifty thousand pounds, however advertising and promotion come out your end."

Mr Brown, disgusted with the deal, placed both hands on his face as if trying to stop it falling off.

"I'll consider your proposition deeply," said old Mr Lame.

"Will we?" asked Mr Brown.

"Books and covers," said old Mr Lame, pointing to his own head.

Channel 54's owner managed to see them to his office door.

"What the hell? How does fifty thousand compare to a million?" screamed Mr Brown.

Young Mr Lame hit the lift for floor seventy-four. Again, his big brother unfolded the scenario to Mr Brown on the journey up.

"Listen, we knew Channel 54 was rubbish. They were called Channel 7, 9, 23 and 51 before, and all declared bankruptcy within months of going into production."

"So why bother going there?"

"Create a bit of friendly fire. Play both sides against one another," said old Mr Lame.

"But Channel 54 isn't even in the same ballpark as Channel 74."

"Yes, but Channel 74 don't know that, do they?" smirked old Mr Lame.

"Oh, that's why we went to Channel 74 earlier to assess their deal?"

"Congratulations. Welcome to the business world."

The lift then reopened on floor seventy-four. If their egos were inflated previously, now the building needed an extension to fit all three arrogant berks. Channel 74's executive shuddered in his office as the pretentious trio blasted his door open.

"Here's our terms and conditions," demanded old Mr Lame.

That's the way the cookie crumbles. Mr Brown and his boys waltzed away with six million over four years exclusively. Boiled down, the Great Eight Chase was worth one point five million every year.

CHAPTER 12

Difference of Opinion & Opinion of Difference 18/1

We've had a healthy mix of continental juggernauts, a blend of charisma, science and efficiency. Now I think it's time I served up the best of the rest. And something was rumbling in Dublin. Ireland has always been renowned for rearing traditional thoroughbreds, highly capable horses. But in all its years of foaling animals, never before had two genuine stars come along at once.

A mare giving birth to twins is rare, a ten thousand to one shot. So when Difference of Opinion and Opinion of Difference entered the world in 2010, the Irish racing universe came to a standstill.

"Twins!" declared the vet, to the surprise of owner Mr O'Neil.

"Are they both boys?" asked Mr O'Neil.

"Girl and boy, best of both. Brother and sister combo."

Difference of Opinion and Opinion of Difference were blossoming through the Irish winter, soaking up new techniques. It aided their growth being siblings; family always comes first after all. I'm going to have to abbreviate their names, so the stallion Difference of Opinion will now be referred to as Doo, and his sister Opinion of Difference is Ood. They could also be told apart because Doo had a white spot on the bridge of his nose.

The happy-go-lucky pair played relentlessly during the off season. Mr O'Neil encouraged their childish behaviour; all work and no play isn't a good formula. Mr O'Neil's vast wealth came from a fleet of bouncy castles. He had kids jumping and bumping from Dublin to Cork. But horse racing was his real passion, and owning two near identical thoroughbreds gave him obvious marketability.

"You two are the apple of my eye," he'd say on regular visits to the stables.

"What does he mean by apples?" asked Doo.

"I'm not entirely sure, and I don't appreciate the weird look in his eyes," replied Ood.

The twin horses were freaked out by Mr O'Neil's devotion and loving body language. It got to the point where he slept in a vacant stable opposite them. The man fussed about their saddles and the combs used to brush their coats.

"Be gentle. Treat them like graceful lords of the track," he'd order.

Having an overbearing parent can be annoying, but for a horse receiving extraordinary attention contributes to their sense of worth.

"Who's the faster out of the two?" inquired Mr O'Neil.

"Odds as even really, one day Difference of Opinion by an inch, the next day Opinion of Difference takes the bragging rights," explained the trainer.

"Equal in speed as well," said Mr O'Neil.

Doo and Ood were so inseparable they organised who was to finish in front beforehand. They'd alternate each training day.

"Maybe in the heat of a race that'll determine a true number one," wondered Mr O'Neil.

Their debut happened in Laytown; they had the home field advantage over other competitors.

The duo settled into the stalls, preparing to unleash fun and excitement into racing.

"Who should win the first race?" asked Ood.

"Ladies first," flapped Doo.

Doo and Ood left the pedestrian horses for dead. A clear two lengths separated them. But as promised, Ood took the victory by a length from her brother. A reef and ribbon were placed over her neck. Doo glanced at the total adulation being heaped on his sister; jealousy crept into the back of his mind.

Back at the stables the siblings reconciled their friendship, although Mr O'Neil bestowed special treatment on Ood and stroked her a little more.

"Daddy's girl," snarled Doo.

"Don't be like this. When you win he'll give you lots of attention."

Doo stayed silent. He contemplated whether sacrificing his personal success was worth it. He'd sleep on it and come to a decisive answer on whether to go further as planned.

For another three races their agreement was honoured; however, underneath Doo grew impatient. His second place finishes became ever closer. Unbeknownst to him his relentless attitude pushed on Ood; she progressed quickly and soon could actually match her older brother stride for stride.

"I think the girl is a different class, smoother and more relaxed," said Mr O'Neil.

"The lad is a bit rough and tumble, granted, but for pure ability his sister couldn't touch him," responded the trainer.

"She runs with glamour and pace."

"Speed and power any day, time or place," argued the trainer.

They discussed the various qualities of each animal in specifics until sunset. Trainer and owner agreed to disagree.

Race five pitted the two horses in Ireland's greatest thoroughbred competition the Irish Epic. One mile, the ultimate straight flatland, a race event many owners dream of winning.

In all relationships, there's a turning point, and the Irish Epic was the one that upset the apple cart. Now, if you're following, Ood was supposed to take the title. A selfish streak washed over her brother.

They galloped away as per, bro and sis stroking off into the distance. Ood led comfortably even though she heard the battering of hooves behind her. Yard by yard Doo reeled her in; he'd live on her shoulder if he needed to.

"What's happening bro? You're my eyes and ears."

"They've found a second wind," he explained.

Nothing of the sort; most horses had conceded and were practically jogging.

Doo galloped alongside his sister.

"I'd have been trapped if I didn't come alongside," he said.

The finishing post was in sight. Doo amped up his pace, nudging ahead and stealing the crown.

Tension arrived by the truckload between the two. They were no longer on speaking terms; stable nights were interesting to put it mildly. Fuelled by spite and revenge, Ood sulked around their home. Her brother avoided her, a wise decision.

"So much for brotherly love," she fumed.

"We might be twins, but there's only room for one champion." He showed no sign of apologising.

"We had an arrangement, you're greedy and FYI I'm all the racer you are."

Doo slyly chuckled, "Even on my worst day you couldn't hang onto my tail."

A fiery glare appeared in her eyes. "Listen bro, you stole the Irish Epic from under my nose. I'll beat you anytime, anyplace."

"I've been holding back in cruise control not to hurt your precious feelings."

"Next outing one on one, no holds barred," vented Ood.

"It's your funeral sis."

The heated debate finished and both horses raged inside. Race six wouldn't be for four weeks, plenty of time to sharpen their tools for arguably the most hotly anticipated battle on Irish soil. As days were ticked off the calendar, their demeanour altered. They trained on separate schedules, and hourly feeding had to be modified.

"Did you see the way Difference of Opinion organised himself on the shoulder? His intelligent thoroughbred sister could learn a thing or two," blabbed the trainer.

"She was a little unaware, I'll give you that," said Mr O'Neil.

"He's starting to emerge as top stallion, winning two on the bounce."

"You might very well be right." Mr O'Neil seemed slightly flat about his favoured girl.

The day of reckoning loomed, and each horse was unsure who held an edge. When let out of the stalls, brother and sister went hell for leather, bumbling and barrelling into one another, veering off. Circuit jockeys roughly tugged the reins, keeping them in line. Their unprofessional antics left them in seventh and eighth place.

Soon the infighting became a regular procedure. They sabotaged their own success. Although both knew this war was destructive, neither wanted to be the first to make amends.

"This is an utter kerfuffle," groaned Mr O'Neil.

"Something's got to be done. Yesterday he tried to break down her stables."

"What a headache! It's too expensive to have two losing horses."

"Which one will you keep?" the trainer asked.

Mr O'Neil, somewhat saddened by the reality one had to go, never responded.

Doo and Ood hobbled into their stables at night; physically they were at sixes and sevens, taking numerous hours to nod off. Their feud generated a negative output in performance. Four races passed without a single podium. As quick as a rat up a drainpipe, the brother and sister novelty wore off. Fans stopped caring. One minute you're toast of Ireland, the next you're being heckled and booed.

Mr O'Neil had fallen out of love with his able but unwilling children – no more stable sleepovers. Only one race remained for the unruly twosome, a steeplechase in Tipperary, a personal favourite for both. Winner and runner-up gained automatic entry to the Chase. Before the race Ood and Doo mutually decided not to interfere and let their racing do the talking.

Ood sneaked it by a whisker from Doo; however there were no hard feelings.

Disastrously Mr O'Neil negotiated the sale of one of his twins to a local glue factory, following whatever the outcome was of the Chase. Think of that when you next use a Prittstick.

CHAPTER 13

Black Sheep 250/1

Bringing up the rear is our eighth participant; saving the best till last, I give you Black Sheep. The steed's name was an excellent joke because he was neither black nor a sheep. Actually his coat was a bright snowy white with long straight white hair; excluding Long Wait, he'd have been the prettiest horse. But looks aren't everything. You have to account for personality, intelligence and body type before selecting a thoroughbred.

The stud hailed from London, home of Buckingham Palace and the Houses of Parliament. Just because London was his main address didn't mean Black Sheep wasn't firmly acquainted with the beauty of England.

His owners were, for want of a better term, part of a travelling community. They'd travel around England sightseeing, using Black Sheep to pull a cart through fields. For him it was entirely peaceful rolling along the foothills, and green grass made him appreciate nature. Black Sheep didn't do that much to earn his keep, and the owners were kind hearted and friendly towards him. It seemed the stallion had his life paved in gold.

Life has a funny way of turning things on its head, sending you down a path you never intended on. It was a usual Monday morning at the campsite. Leaves followed the wind adoringly, and the sun shone crisp and vibrant. Black Sheep awoke to this glorious scene day after day, but the view never ceased to amaze him. Although when he peeked at his owners on this day, a frantic, scrambling worry glossed their faces.

"Why would you tell him where we live?" asked the female owner.

"He isn't a man to be messing around," the male frowned.

Black Sheep couldn't think of what had them flustered. They raced about, attaching the steed's trailer to their vehicle. They shoved the key into the ignition, powering up the diesel engine, immediately pulling off. The trailer rattled over the lumps and bumps of the fields.

"Oh dear," said the man, stopping the vehicle.

"Time to face the music, hubby," replied the wife.

As clean as a whistle, a white four by four blocked the exit.

"If this goes belly up, I want you to know, I blame you for everything bad that's happened," announced his wife.

"Doesn't surprise me one bit."

The four by four seemed aggressive. It had been lowered and modified with an enormous chrome grille, which gave you a sense the jeep growled rather than revved. Out came the driver, a brute of a man. Those thick legs operated his brawny torso, and he walked with authority.

"Maybe they'll just talk," prayed the male.

"He isn't the talking sort; I think he goes straight to breaking."

He shuffled to the passenger side, opening the door for his boss Mr Williams. A man who also went by 'Whack 'Em Up' Williams or 'Willing and Killing' Williams. By all accounts, he wasn't classified as a gangster; more like a businessman with underhand tactics. He stepped out in his spotless leather shoes and pinstripe suit. He had a scar spanning his forehead and a sovereign ring on his pinkie finger.

"You've been ducking my calls," Mr Williams spoke in a menacing grunt.

"Low battery. I was heading to a pay phone," squeaked the male.

"I'll save you the trouble, where's my cash?" Mr Williams shoved his tie into his shirt. No need to get it stained with blood.

"Mr Williams, are you getting younger? You must tell me your secret."

Flattery won't get you everywhere. Mr Williams looked fierce; his associate threw him a nine iron golf club.

"I love golf me, one nil, two nil, three nil," said Mr Williams, strapping on a pair of white gloves; they aid grip and give a cleaner-swinging follow-through.

"I think golf is scored in par. The less shots the better," explained the man.

"Are you insulting me? Are you calling me thick?" His voice vibrated in anger.

"I think that's exactly what he's doing, trying to mug you about," added his partner.

Mr Williams' irritation levels rose. He began blowing out his cheeks.

"I'm no genius, Mr Williams. I mean no ill will towards you sir." The male appealed to Mr Williams' human side.

"Can't let him off so lightly boss, got a reputation to uphold."

Mr William hurled the club, crashing it into their windscreen. Multiple cracks fanned across the glass.

"Have I made a statement?" he asked.

The stocky hired muscle nodded approvingly.

"Good, now back to the money you owe."

The man trembled in despair and his mouth remained wide open like a hungry hippo.

"The damage to my car isn't cheap to fix."

What was the damage? So it would seem yesterday afternoon the male traveller hadn't judged the turning circle of his campervan correctly. And Mr Williams' jeep was parked on the high street. As the camper spun it accidentally grazed the white paint job, slightly denting the bumper. Even 'slightly' might be an overstatement. Mr Williams saw this opportunity to exploit the situation and grabbed it with both hands. When I say both hands, I mean he throttled the male until his face arrived at a rare sky-blue colour. By then, Black Sheep's owner was willing to do anything asked of him.

"We settled on five k," said Mr Williams, retrieving his club from the windscreen.

"I don't have that sort of money, and very much doubt I'll ever see it."

"Tell me you're joking. Cause if not this doesn't have a picture book ending for you."

Mr Williams' fearsome thug popped the boot. There was a sinister silence as if trees, bushes and hedges anticipated a violent episode.

"Give me a week, I'll sell my campervan," bargained the male.

"And where will we sleep?" asked his wife.

"Really! Sleeping arrangements are the least of our worries."

Mr Williams rolled up both sleeves above the elbow. He switched from golf glove to a pair of brass knuckledusters. "Are you hungry? Cause I have a knuckle sandwich with your name on it."

"What if I told you there was a way you could achieve more than the five k we agreed on, would you be interested?"

"Start making sense or else."

The man swivelled his eyes nervously.

Neigh! Black Sheep didn't adore being locked in a trailer during daytime.

"A horse! Every man wishes to own one," said the man convincingly.

They walked over to Black Sheep's trailer.

"He's magnificent, a glorious steed, very loyal and under-standing," exalted the female owner.

Mr Williams' associate muttered something into his ear. Whatever the words, Mr Williams took no further persuading. Deeds were signed over, and Black Sheep had new owners. The steed's long pathway of gold hit the skids rapidly.

The serenity of a stroll about the countryside was killed. He now lived in a grotty broken down stable; you know it's disgusting when bacteria are growing on the wild mushrooms. Black Sheep, for the first time, was dictated to. He ate, slept and breathed racing. Trainer after trainer battled to teach him and improvements were nonexistent; he was stuck in his ways.

"It's like pushing a rock up a hill wearing ice skates," one trainer moaned.

"Try harder, boy, or else," Mr Williams screamed at the steed.

"Speak in a less commanding tone. Remember you got him at a late stage of his racing life," said the trainer.

Black Sheep was ten years old. At best, barring injury and a healthy diet, he could probably run two to three years max.

"Just cut your losses. You win some you lose some boss," conceded his associate.

"Why can't he run?" asked Mr Williams.

"Obviously he runs. It's his bone structure, muscle mass and balance is way off," explained the trainer.

"So you're saying his muscles are too small for his frame."

"Yes, I'd liken it to putting a motorbike engine into a lorry."

This made Mr Williams develop a crooked smile. Well, when your jaw's been broken four times you might find it hard too.

"If he gains extra muscle he has the potential to be a beast," exclaimed Mr Williams.

"What's on your mind?" asked his associate curiously.

"I think a trip to the vets is in order," grinned Mr Williams.

Black Sheep's transformation was utterly startling. After two months, with a helping hand from a vet, he became absolutely shredded. Deep cuts of muscle were barely contained by his coat.

Now a weight training programme on this level may have few drawbacks, namely, unpredictability, aggression and nightmares; for stallion and jockeys alike.

"That's my kind of horse, he'll terrify his competitors," said Mr Williams, glowing.

Black Sheep frightened horses and race fans, and jockeys dreaded hopping on his bulging back. All but one jockey; Mr Steeds is the name, horse racing is his game and claim to fame. With a self-given title, he assumed a villainous role around the paddock. So having an evil-looking monster of a horse went hand in hand. Mr Steeds wore a black face mask like a wannabe Zorro.

Mr Williams saw how much nastier and savage Black Sheep looked.

"Now don't be kind with the whip, his legs will take it," ordered Mr Williams.

"What have you been feeding him?" wondered Mr Steeds.

"Never you mind; all you need to do is remember the whip is there for whipping," Mr Williams restated.

The terrifying duo set upon a mission to demolish Britain's race circuit. The roughhouse tactics delivered eight straight victories, all because no horse or jockey wanted to get within a mile radius of Black Sheep. He even did an unprecedented double of the National and the Cup. So a treble including the Great Eight Chase would be preposterous.

Living in the UK as a spectacle like the Chase flourished from promotional hype and attention, Mr Williams convinced himself that Black Sheep should be England's lone representative. And he didn't hesitate to zoom down to meet Old Mr Lame for a chinwag at his office.

"The pride of England, my horse Black Sheep, deserves to honour his country," said Mr Williams.

Old Mr Lame hadn't heard of Mr Williams' street cred and chose to be abrasive.

"Lots of jumped up men boast to me about their animals, but for you to barge into my office shouting the odds ... are you crazy?" replied Old Mr Lame.

"Look my boy has done the double, the National and the Cup. Nobody does that these days."

"Impressive; however the last qualifying race takes place in Argentina."

Mr Williams stood puzzled. "So what are you saying exactly?"

"Well, unless your horse has wings and can fly to Argentina in two hours and win the race then you're flat out of luck."

"So is it a no, then?" asked Mr Williams.

"Lock the door on the way out," said Old Mr Lame, winking.

Gangsters have a unique habit of getting their own way. Within forty-eight hours of their initial meeting, Black Sheep filled out the line-up.

Did Mr Lame have a change of heart?

To a certain degree. He was delicately informed by an associate of Mr Williams how arduous it is to walk with broken legs and write with snapped fingers and how falling out of a moving vehicle might be super painful.

CHAPTER 14

Uncle Frank

Let's have a quick run-through of where we are so far. Stadium check, television station check, horses check, jockeys check, betting houses double check. Then let the awful race commence. Punters, my faithful customer base, where would I be without them? Right here I suppose.

They say you can pick your friends but not your family. Now every family has that one lazy, silly Billy person with his idiotic get-rich-quick scheme. I introduce to you Uncle Frank.

Uncle Frank was overall a harmless fella. He took everything with a pinch of salt. His joking character made him a favourite amongst his nieces and nephews, but not adults. A lot of family gatherings he'd been barred from attending for setting a bad example. As we know, nobody's perfect. I'm pretty close, but we all have our flaws. Uncle Frank's biggest hindrance was a wicked gambling habit, which affected him badly. To date I've taken upwards of one hundred thousand pounds off him over the past fifteen years. Hey, better me than drink and cigarettes, that stuff will kill you. I'll just keep you poor and miserable.

Uncle Frank's gambling addiction couldn't be quenched. He dreamt of one day hitting the big time. My rules for these sorts of people are, as long as you pay then, please! Please! Bet away. Uncle Frank had gambled money borrowed from friends and family, to the point of no return. Only his younger brother still spoke to him. As children, Frank used to protect him. His younger brother lived an average life; he had a wonderful wife, four beautiful children and ran his own plumbing company. He never forgot the early days when Frank stopped people hurting him and always felt his success was mostly due to him.

They'd meet at a local bar since his wife refused to let Frank step foot in their home. One too many ales at Christmas and he'd wind up saying something horrific.

"Brother, how're you keeping?" asked Uncle Frank.

"Taking it one day at a time," answered his younger brother, bringing over two pints of bitter.

"Is the family good though?" Uncle Frank loved his nieces and nephews limitlessly. On his few uncommon winning days he'd buy them a present.

"Yeah, everyone's happy, working hard." He took out his wallet, showing him pictures of the kids.

"Wow! Look at how much they've grown."

"Sure you'll have it one day," suggested his little brother.

There was a weird silence, an awkward quietness. Sadly the pair understood Uncle Frank had already given up.

"Maybe in the future," Frank said doubtfully.

At the bookies, you have a steady flow of customers, and soon enough friendly connections form. Frank's losing partner was a man called Lee, who paid for my house, cars and yearly holiday. God bless him.

"So Frank, what are you doing with yourself?" asked his brother, hoping for a positive answer.

"A bit of this and that, keeping my head up." Translation: he was doing nothing at all, pretending to be happy.

Lee spotted Uncle Frank's slaphead shining off the LED lighting.

"Frankie me old mucker," Lee said, pulling up a stool.

"Lee boy, what have you heard?" replied Frank.

Lee referred to himself as an octopus because he seemed to have a reach far beyond his means.

"This Saturday! The Great Eight Chase! Are you ready?" he asked hysterically.

Uncle Frank gulped his beer. He could sense his brother awaiting his response. "Nah, gambling ain't for me."

"Come off it lad, you'll be there Saturday placing a healthy wager."

"Gambling ruined my life. Cost me way more than money," Uncle Frank stated.

His brother thought this might be Uncle Frank turning over a new leaf. Dream on; once a gambler, always a gambler.

Lee swigged his stout, creating a foamy beard. "OK, say you were to bet. Who would you fancy?"

"I'm not remotely interested in it."

"Look I'm not asking you to put money on it," said Lee, wiping away his foamy moustache.

Uncle Frank had a system. He'd pick the horse by closing his eye and letting his finger guide him. Only something magnificent like the Chase deserved special commitment.

"Vintage Red unbeaten and hot favourite."

"Wrong!"

"Something Good then, formidable standing he has."

"Wrong! Wrong!"

"Long Wait, she has great technique and is going through a purple patch," Uncle Frank said expertly. And he'd suggested he wasn't keen on betting.

"Wrong! Wrong! Wrong," responded Lee, making the sound for an incorrect buzzer.

"I surrender, who's gonna win?"

"The yanks are coming," nodded Lee.

Uncle Frank peered at the newspaper, searching for the American participant.

"Heartbreaker, really? The record isn't one of virtue and pride."

Lee tapped his nose, implying he had inside information.

"Heartbreaker comes alive on the biggest of stages."

"But Vintage Red and Something Good are stunning stallions, miles above the field," interrupted Frank's younger brother.

Lee and Frank stared at his brother in shock.

"Where is this knowledge coming from, the interweb?" wondered Frank.

"People talk," he replied, "so what gives you the inside track?"

"Friend of a friend," Lee pointed to a guy at the bar who gingerly walked over with his head on a swivel.

"And you are?" speculated the younger brother.

"No names. I was told by you no names," said the man, pushing down his baseball cap.

"Relax, you're amongst respectable men," said Lee.

The men sat sipping their pints listening to the dodgy guy spell out his theory.

"Look I'm an American native myself. I live in Austin, Texas, not far from Heartbreaker's ranch."

Although he acted private, the man divulged a lot of info from his long family tree.

"It relates to country size, out of all the thoroughbreds Heartbreaker comes from an enormous nation in comparison. So racing in England will be a piece of pie. At eight to one, it's a steal if we pool all our money together. Sit back and watch my America compatriot do the business."

"I don't know, sounds a hint too iffy," announced Uncle Frank's brother, leaving the table.

"You're in Frankie, right?"

"Couldn't pass up this opportunity, could I?" Uncle Frank added his hundred pounds to the pot.

As Uncle Frank gambled away his week's shopping money, his younger brother, slightly tipsy, stumbled home. As he wandered around the back streets the alcohol began stirring his imagination. The moon, which is usually round, morphed into a broken heart, and stars spelled out the word Heartbreaker. He saw heartbroken houses, heartbroken cars driven by heartbroken people.

It was all too much to absorb. He sprinted home. But peculiarly, his heartbroken home wasn't a safe haven either.

He rushed to his heartbroken bed, sleeping off the illusions. The following morning he awoke to the poignant strains of Mariah Carey's classic song 'Heartbreaker'.

"Turn it off love," he shouted.

"Why? You're not the heartbreaking kind are you?" she said, dancing.

At that moment, his four kids joined in, singing the chorus and jumping on the bed. The man had no alternative. The wife and kids screaming 'heartbreaker' from each and every last vocal cord made it abundantly clear.

So that very same afternoon, as I tucked into my beef baguette, an unfamiliar man entered Bet Your Life On It.

"Greetings my man, how may you require my service?" I asked.

He appeared jittery, like a moth enticed by the light yet sceptical over if it was a wise decision to engage. "I'd like to make a bet," he whispered.

"Bet on what? Horses, greyhounds, sports? Pick your poison."

"Horses, the Great Eight Chase specifically."

"Seen a lot of action on the Chase. Vintage Red is it?"

"Let me put fifty on Heartbreaker," he murmured.

"The American. Odd choice. Black Sheep is my pick, homegrown. Not sure how Heartbreaker will fare on foreign soil. Then again, fifty pence is hardly breaking the bank."

The man clammed up; his Adam's apple quivered. "Not fifty pence, fifty k," he confirmed.

"Fifty k?!" I almost choked to death on my baguette.

"Yes!"

His stake was confirmed by way of debit card, wiping out his savings account. Fifty grand on an eight to one steed gave him a return of erm . . . four hundred thousand quid.

Since the race is just a chapter or two away, you should place your bets now.

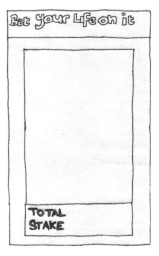

CHAPTER 15

The Stables

At 7.30, a tremendous scene set the Manchester evening abuzz. All eight finely trained championship thoroughbreds were being led into the stables. The world's top media searched for interviews and pictures of coaches and owners, who duly obliged, lapping up their fifteen minutes of fame.

Bitter rivals Mr Philip and Mr Vladimir posed for a photo op. Both billionaires wore shoes with thick soles, trying to seek a height advantage.

Vintage Red and Something Good mainly spent their stable time sizing up the competition. However, their two disloyal owners occupied all their attention, signing autographs for hoards of fans, which inflamed them.

"We do all the work and they soak up the glory," seethed Vintage Red.

"Traitors, they vow to be honest, to care about you. Within seconds, you're shoved out into the cold," said a betrayed Something Good.

106

"I hear you brother," agreed Vintage Red, who was receiving admiring glances from an infatuated professor.

"So this is Mr Red. What a sumptuous creature." The professor had pleaded for golden girl Long Wait to be located next door.

"My steed is in fantastic form, anything less than first he'll have to walk home," Mr Philip joked.

The professor, so attracted to Vintage Red's frame and jet black coat, edged towards his bars. The stallion stared in alarm at the professor's mannerisms.

"Don't mind if I check out his backside, do you?" asked the professor, unlocking the stable door.

"I beg your pardon?" raged a freaked Mr Philip.

"No, it's not what you think, by adjusting their back shoes I can get five miles per hour more out of my girl." The professor dug his fingers into his right palm.

Mr Philip prohibited him from entering Vintage's stable. "I'm going to get a restraining order against you. Stalking a horse, what's wrong with you man?"

The doolally professor shrugged. He accepted the love connection was up to Long Wait's feminine appeal.

"Be on your best behaviour, and don't be shy. Vintage Red wants to be friends."

Long Wait had a gander at the steed, but he wasn't her type.

A race official called time on the stable festivities. The barn was bolted shut. And with the horses estimated to be worth a combined thirty-nine million pounds, they were guarded by twenty-four-hour security units.

Focusing on a race can take a lot of emotional energy. Stallions and mares mostly concentrate on happier, relaxing days after competing to get by. Silence surrounded the stalls and spite graced the atmosphere. Nothing More's gimpy leg wobbled, Vintage felt bitter, Something Good rather sour, Doo and Ood unwavering sorrow, Long Wait forced, Heartbreaker was fascinated by knowing there are other countries besides America and Black Sheep avoided sleep like the plague to ward off nightmares.

"I do believe this is the most marvellous stable one's ever slept in," said Heartbreaker.

Claudio Rossi's design wasn't limited to the track. His handiwork on the barn was totally evident. There was a glass skylight that allowed in lavish amounts of moonlight. Sturdy pinewood pillars crafted each stall, filled with barrels of fresh hay. Handcrafted iron gates glossed in shimmering silver.

When can I move in?

"Why is everyone down in the dumps? England's so exquisite," cheered Heartbreaker.

Seven pairs of eyes savagely glared at his chipper exterior.

"Will the Queen be here tomorrow? I've always wanted to meet Queen Elizabeth," Heartbreaker clamoured. "The Great Eight Chase, this is where I define my moniker as unequivocally the greatest."

"Oh, silly little mustang, you're just here to make up numbers," responded Black Sheep.

"Or to get American spectators involved," added Ood.

"On the contrary, I'm ripped and ready to rock," Heartbreaker said in a defiant tone.

"Nobody's beating me on my patch. I'll be victorious come what may," affirmed Black Sheep; his extraordinary weight gain had doctored his voice to a higher note.

"That's as long as you don't blow up beforehand."

"Hey Heartbeat or whatever your name is. I'm what a real horse looks like." Black Sheep flexed, those deep ridges of muscles popping on his back.

"So you've hit the gym, big deal. What else you got?" said an unconvinced Doo.

"It's all I need."

"You're just hype, all bluster and no bite. Winning races on fear doesn't hold merit," clarified Doo.

This game of verbal tennis takes place in all barns; it's called the storm before the storm. While several of the animals enjoyed the argy-bargy, top horses Vintage Red and Something Good gazed at Nothing More, writhing in sheer torment.

109

"Nothing More, girl, are you feeling OK?" asked Something Good, stretching his head out of his stall.

"Yikes, that surely isn't healthy," said Vintage, staring at her leg.

The leg twitched and was skinny in comparison to the other three.

"I tore my tendon in training weeks ago performing a jump," she grimaced.

"So why haven't they pulled you out?" quizzed Long Wait.

"Money, I guess. Their greed won't let me heal properly."

The nattering between Heartbreaker and Black Sheep halted. Sympathy for Nothing More consumed their hearts.

"Something's got to be done. They can't get away with this," fumed Long Wait.

"What can we do though? They own us," replied a defeated Nothing More.

The horses debated options, but a way to gain revenge appeared nonexistent. If they sabotaged the Great Eight Chase, their owners might discard them.

"I'm willing to sacrifice my win for the benefit of us all," announced Vintage Red.

"Arrogant aren't we? I suspect you're afraid Something Good might have your number," grinned Heartbreaker.

Vintage Red never got intimidated by opponents, such was the pristine record he had attained. And forfeiting his unblemished ranking would most definitely kill his world roadshow.

"I'll resign a chance at the title," agreed Something Good; quite frankly being jilted by Mr Vladimir tainted his racing mindset.

"I'm in too," smiled Long Wait. She knew, win or lose, she'd be used for producing babies anyway.

Twins Doo and Ood complied with the general ruling. Heartbreaker and Black Sheep also consented, not wanting to be the odd ones out.

"No. I refuse to win by default, fair and square or not at all." Nothing More didn't appreciate handouts.

Then an idea struck Vintage Red, like a dart stabbing the bullseye. "What if we all won?"

"How can we all win?" said a confused Heartbreaker.

"If we cross the winning post at exactly the same moment, we all finish first," Vintage explained.

The horses remained silent, digesting his brilliant notion.

"That way we'll all win; and bookies will lose a bucket load of dosh, one trillion to be precise," said Something Good.

"And because none of us are hunting for victory we can stroll along," stated Long Wait.

Each horse dozed off to sleep comfortable, calm and content. But tomorrow, when race day arrived, would all horses toe the line?

CHAPTER 16

They're Off

Full of electric excitement, Mrs Brown's racetrack was declared open. The red tape had been cut by the local mayor. Mr Brown became a small-time hero, hitting back for independent businesses.

Young and Old Mr Lame attached themselves to the rich and famous in their private box, rubbing shoulders with rugby stars, singers, TV presenters and actors.

"How did we do this?" asked a flabbergasted Young Mr Lame.

Old Mr Lame observed the elegantly manufactured racecourse as the 3.30 steeplechase got underway.

"Sometimes things are just meant to be," Old Mr Lame said, patting his brother's shoulder.

They popped the cork on some vintage vino supplied by Mr Philip.

"To good money and their money," they toasted.

Mr and Mrs Brown were busy with a meet and greet. A documentary crew followed them, detailing the glamorous occasion for a TV programme. Mrs Brown acted in an entirely different style around the extended film crew. She held her husband's hand and wore a significantly revealing red lace dress. Fame converts normal people into desperate monsters.

"They love us, hubby," beamed Mrs Brown, waving to the jam-packed audience.

"And to think you weren't on board initially," said Mr Brown.

"You were right; I didn't have your vision. In the future, I won't question the decisions you make."

Mr Brown did twirls, cartwheels, star jumps and gambols internally.

"Stick with me honey. I mean, what could possibly go wrong?" boasted Brown.

Hold that thought, because the time for talking was over. National anthems were sung for the represented countries. Jockeys mounted their able but annoyed horses. One hundred and seven thousand, five hundred and sixty seven spectators' hearts leaped out of their chests as Vintage Red and co descended onto the course.

"Does everyone remember the strategy?" whispered Vintage Red.

"Yes, we let Nothing More be the frontrunner. And then claw her in down the final furlong," replied Heartbreaker. "The Queen, the Queen."

"That's not the Queen, it's just a woman in an enormous hat," said Black Sheep.

"Don't get distracted. If we execute correctly, they'll never live this down," said Vintage Red.

Eighteen months in the making, thousands of man-hours sunk into the project. Millions in construction and legal costs, one bizarre Italian designer later and here we were. Race fever swept the crowd, and their seats were left vacant. The Great Eight Chase isn't a race you watch from an armchair.

The racecourse turf was inspected and concluded to be good to soft in places. A dry couple of nights had firmed up the soil. I'll hand the proceedings over to your commentator, Curtis Bell.

"Hello and welcome to the first ever the Great Eight Chase sponsored by Tick-Tock Clocks. A balmy afternoon prevails over the racecourse. The main event a tantalising three-mile conclusion to a monumental race weekend here in Manchester.

"A thriller is in store. Expect a cautious start from Vintage Red, his calculated approach will serve him fantastically. Something Good hugs the inside rail, he'll keep a watchful eye on his French adversary, while Nothing More racing in the blue tendon socks huddles into the middle. They're called into line – remember it's a rolling start. And they're off, a blistering eruption throbs out of the elevated fans. I can't hear myself think over the thundering echo; however Nothing More holds a slight advantage although she doesn't look so agile heading into jump one. Give this girl an inch and she'll take it, but will she have enough to see her home? Vintage Red and Something Good surprisingly bring up the rear. The pace is uninspiring. Long Wait lies in second while the beefed up late entry Black Sheep currently sits in third, trailed by Difference of Opinion and Opinion of Difference, keeping American boy Heartbreaker at bay."

The two favourites were polar opposites of their Russian and French wealthy owners. They got along like peas in a pod. Plodding together in perfect tranquillity, chilling out. Seeing their agenda blossoming capped it all.

"Something Good, have you ever heard of a place called the Five Fields of Freedom?"

"Yeah, supposedly old retired horses live in luxury there."

Their jockeys weren't used to this level of laziness; they tugged their harnesses, but neither horse blinked.

"Do you believe it's for real?" asked Vintage Red. Four years had passed since he'd last seen Second to None, and he missed his running buddy.

"Nah, it's one of them old wives' tales," concluded Something Good.

"They're now a third of the race distance and Nothing More ekes out a further lead, she floats over the water jump splashing second-place Long Wait. If anything the speed is actually decreasing, wait we have movement, Heartbreaker has taken fifth, splitting the twins."

"I can't see the royal family anywhere," said Heartbreaker, peering into the bored stiff onlookers.

"Why are you so captivated by the royal family?" questioned Doo.

"It's not every day you meet the Queen, especially being an American ambassador."

Heartbreaker eyeballed every single person, forgetting the game plan and falling to last place.

"Heartbreaker, what are you doing man?" shouted Vintage Red.

"Sorry, I got caught up."

"Heartbreaker's lost his head, slipping to eighth as they tediously glide over another hedge. Nothing More is still leading from Long Wait. Half the race distance covered as Heartbreaker surges past uncharacteristically slow Vintage Red and Something Good."

"Ease up boy, you'll dismantle our system," panicked Something Good.

"It's my momentum."

"Heartbreaker flies over a hurdle knocking on the door of third in the standings of Black Sheep."

"Follow the protocol son," said Black Sheep.

"Heartbreaker begins the charge as we reach the business end of the race. Black Sheep is strangely in with a shout as his bulky body pounds the ground. Difference of Opinion and Opinion of Difference are yet again running identically. Black Sheep's jockey cracks his long raking whip onto the steed's beastly thighs. The English-born horse bolts his vulgar powerhouse frame and kicks up a fuss. Long Wait is swiftly brushed aside and Nothing More is in his sights."

"What's going on?" yelled a frustrated Vintage Red.

"Muscular reflex, it can't be controlled," answered Black Sheep.

"Black Sheep takes the lead with only one and a half miles separating the two hundred and fifty to one outsider from an unforeseen victory."

"It's all going to pot," exclaimed Long Wait.

"Terminate agreement. May the best horse win!" announced Heartbreaker.

"They're starting to liven up as Heartbreaker gallops intensely after the leader Black Sheep. Difference of Opinion and Opinion of Difference cut off Vintage Red and Something Good's route, lengthening the gap. The Great Eight Chase has had a much needed kick up the backside. The dynamic animals press into overdrive, soon bypassing fragile former leader Nothing More."

"We're buggered now," said a disgruntled Something Good.

"Scrap it! How about it, you and I display our talents? Duke it out like superstars," Vintage Red offered.

"What a vision to behold Vintage Red and Something Good have switched on the afterburners. Here they come, their thunderous hooves belting the grass as we head into the final quarter, it's going to be a climactic ending. Vintage Red blasts and drives, Something Good swarms and strives, visibly both steeds are on a mission."

"They look furious," said Ood, seeing Vintage swallow up their lead.

"You rotten scumbags, we had an arrangement," said Something Good, snatching fifth place.

"Vintage Red is pouring it on thick and heavy. He's now showcasing the reason why he's considered the most thorough of thoroughbreds, breezing to third. Something Good's grit and attitude chip away at fourth-place Long Wait. Soon Heartbreaker will have company, a one-mile shootout is sure to transpire. Black Sheep's leading margin remains stable."

"You lying rascal, what happened to unity?" exclaimed Vintage Red.

"Heartbreaker is being tracked like a hunted fox."

"Tell Black Sheep he upset the formal agreement," said Heartbreaker.

"That doesn't excuse what you did," raged Something Good.

"No way could Nothing More keep up this speed, and if Black Sheep wins it scuppers our understanding."

"The crowd raises its collective voice with half a mile to go, optimism for a fairy book finish. Can Vintage Red retain his unbeaten tag as Black Sheep begins to run low on juice? He's bridged the gap to twenty lengths."

"What are you waiting for Vintage? Get him," screamed Heartbreaker.

"No, we'll finish second together," said Vintage Red.

"Animated and incensed hawk-eyed punters glow in apprehension. The Great Eight Chase is ultimately living up to its hype."

"How is finishing second worth anything?" inquired Long Wait.

"Black Sheep wins, he's the underdog. His odds were ridiculous, bookies will still lose tons of cash, ten billion to be dead on," said Vintage Red, decelerating.

"I'm not busting a gut to catch him," conceded Something Good.

"The chasing six have suddenly straightened across the field in second place, approaching the final furlong. Nothing More, the durable German, seems to actually be gaining ground."

"Keep striding girl," encouraged Ood.

"The pain is unbearable," she winced.

"Push love, fight through the agony," spurred on the gang.

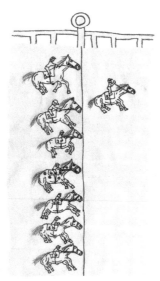

"Extraordinarily Nothing More has re-established herself with the bunch. Their synchronised gallops restore order. Two hundred and fifty to one long shot Black Sheep sails by the winning post, seizing the Great Eight Chase trophy. Winning a one million pound bonus, in a race that failed to materialise. Thank you for joining me in, simply put, a dire demonstration of horse racing."

CHAPTER 17

Post Race Problems

As the dust settled and the smoke cleared, mixed feelings separated each camp. Triumphant Black Sheep rode the success train, albeit a hollow one. Mr Williams basked in a win for the British. Bookies had a terrific outing; Black Sheep was our least backed horse.

The Great Eight horses stormed back to the stables, except for the wonky-legged Nothing More, who limped back. Black Sheep was in full apologetic mode.

"I can't tell you how deeply sorry I am, Vintage Red. Things got out of my hooves," he sighed.

"Selfish git. No honour amongst steeds," snarled Long Wait.

"I have a rare muscle condition, it's unstoppable," said Black Sheep, distressed.

The horses accepted Black Sheep's excuses; nonetheless they knew he'd ruined everything. Vintage Red gave up his throne for a stool.

"Guess we'll be back to our native countries in a few days' time," said Something Good.

"I'll miss this. Over the past night I'd grown to appreciate your company, even Black Sheep," confessed Vintage Red; in France things weren't so rosy.

"What will become of Nothing More?" asked Heartbreaker.

She'd basically collapsed on re-entering her stables; for once Nothing More lived up to her title.

"You're a terrific mare and I'm fortunate to have shared a racetrack with you," flattered Vintage.

Long Wait saw the caring and humble side to Vintage Red. The prime stallion all of a sudden didn't look as ugly.

"I killed it, broke us. I'm a mutant horse, a shambles," cried Black Sheep.

"Don't be down, we'll do it again."

"How, Vintage Red? It's unlikely we'll race each other."

The animals gathered closer together, sticking their heads through their barn doors to listen to Vintage's new idea.

"The idea still holds, all you do is tell your competitors to cross the line at the same time," explained Vintage Red.

"Splendid, soon racing will be outlawed," smiled Something Good.

Outside the barn, a dreadful commotion gained impetus. Mr Williams read the riot act to race administrators.

"You're not testing my horse. He won. Now hand me my prize," he grunted.

The barn door flew open; two race officials stepped over to Black Sheep's stable.

"Lay a hand on his white coat, I'll break your bleeping neck," Mr Williams said politely.

"Sorry, tests are a natural procedure," informed the official, unlocking the stable.

"Test for what? He's built on hay and water."

"Then a blood test will be a breeze."

Mr Williams shot a worried glance towards Black Sheep's husky slabs of flesh. "I won't allow it."

"We have a legally binding contract, my man."

A quiet mumbling chirped out of Mr Williams as he lost his sense of confidence. "Go ahead ... he'll pass with flying colours. How long will it take for test results to come back?"

"Within a day," assured the official.

"I left my phone in my car; need to make a call to my travel agent, estate agent I meant."

The gangster zipped into his car and rocketed down the motorway, chartering a plane abroad. It doesn't take a genius to work out Black Sheep's muscular definition might've been ill-gotten.

Mr Vladimir and Mr Philip marched into the barn boiling with fury. Vintage Red and Something Good had thoroughly dissatisfied their bosses.

"Vintage, my prince, why be like this? I give you the world," Mr Philip sobbed. Vintage coldly turned his back on him.

"Something Good, I brought you from a feeble, weak tramp of a horse to this magnificent stallion. All for you to disappoint in an unbelievable fashion," said Mr Vladimir, weeping and holding onto the barn gates.

Something Good spat hay at his Russian owner.

"You ungrateful dingbat! I'll come in there and tan your behind," he screamed.

Something Good shuffled back a few steps; horse vs human was an all too familiar battle in his life.

"We're finished boy, no more," grumbled Mr Philip.

Vintage Red fluttered dispassionately, and their ties were cut.

Mr Philip wandered away saddened. He hated goodbyes; steeds like Vintage are unique breeds.

"Mr Brown, you do what you want with him."

"Wait Mr Philip. Are you leaving Vintage Red here?"

A pattern took hold quickly. Something Good was ditched, Difference of Opinion and Opinion of Difference, Heartbreaker and Nothing More too.

The weird professor mulled over his decision. With Vintage Red now a free agent, could he be swayed on Long Wait? He judged not.

"Keep Long Wait, she bores me," professed the professor.

Twelve hours after the blood sample, vets were appalled, shocked and amazed a horse could withstand such chemical enhancement. Results revealed Black Sheep had extremely inflated levels of horsepower. Need I say more? Black Sheep had more BHP than a Nissan Gtr. He was ultimately stripped of his victory. And the championship had to be handed to second place, Vintage Red, Something Good, Long Wait, Nothing More, Heartbreaker, Doo and Ood.

Before the news filtered down to us on the ground about Black Sheep, every man and his dog who had pledged a wager on him came skipping along. There was ten billion down the pan. Conversation escalated, and bookmakers had to dole out a further nine hundred and ninety billion bet on the seven promoted winners. Uncle Frank's brother, so excited, had a tattoo of Heartbreaker inked on his chest.

A scandal so public hit front and back pages, lit up the internet for weeks and obliterated the Great Eight Chase. Mr Brown's devastated face pondered his next step. The TV company had pulled out, along with sponsors. Young and Old Mr Lame began distancing themselves from the fiasco, but Mr Brown persisted until they finally returned one of his calls. They arranged to meet at the racetrack.

"I have eight horses to look after, plus a nagging wife and times that by no income equals . . . Catastrophic problems."

Old Mr Lame said sternly, "What's that got to do with us?"

"We're business partners, I need advice."

"You're mistaken, we were business partners. However in our contract it states, should there be a change in circumstances, Lame investments can at any stage opt out," he explained.

"You mean?"

"Adios amigo (Spanish for goodbye friend)," said Old Mr Lame, waving.

The sun covered her face from Mr Brown's misery as he let grey and black storm clouds shelter his universe.

Mrs Brown's racecourse was seen as creepy, and labelled 'the death track'. Husband and wife ambled around the course confused, woeful and bang out of luck.

"Do you think the supermarket offer still stands?" asked Mrs Brown.

"Should've snapped their hand off. At least I have you darling," Mr Brown lovingly responded, kissing her on the forehead.

They chuckled because in a helpless situation, all you can do is laugh. Giggles are always free. The Browns quite enjoyed having eight horses around. After trading away all their livestock, Vintage and his famous seven made alluring companions, and wouldn't have to be slaughtered for profits. Regrettably, money dried up like a closed-down well.

At zero hour, when Mr Brown prepared to sell his land for a fraction of the price, an enormous articulated lorry rolled up outside the barn. Its wheels screeched as it braked.

"Are you expecting visitors?" inquired Mr Brown.

His wife sipped her mug of coffee.

"I don't like surprises," he said as he sweated.

A refined gentleman slipped out of the lorry. His chummy appearance helped settle Mr Brown's nerves.

"Mr Brown, the man with a plan," joked the lorry driver.

"What are you here for?" barked Mr Brown.

The man pointed to the barn, "Walk with me."

Mr Brown guided him to the stables, and the guy whistled as they walked. He was one of those sorts of people who are constantly in an exceptional mood. Tell him an asteroid is about to decimate planet Earth, he'd somehow find a positive.

"Your wife explained. You have eight horses you're trying to offload."

"So, what have you?"

"Consider it done. I'm here for the Great Eight," he squealed.

"Where will they be heading?" asked a concerned Mr Brown, sliding the barn open.

"They're heading for freedom, Mr Five Fields of Freedom," beamed Mr Freedom.

The horses, geed up by a new beginning, neighed for hours.

"I do believe this is what was agreed upon," said Mr Freedom, giving Mr Brown a cheque for well north of one million.

"Need assistance getting them on your wagon?"

"That'll be grand."

Assistance was unnecessary; each thoroughbred galloped onto the trailer merrily, almost bringing a close to this chapter.

Mr and Mrs Brown weren't out the woods yet; they still had an empty stadium. But five minutes after the horses left, a coach pulled up. One hundred and seventy passengers filed out, paying ten pounds to view the arena, which effectively ended horse racing. Millions of tourist folk went there weekly, generating a tidy profit. Mr Brown bought himself a riding lawnmower. Admittedly no combine harvester, but what is?

CHAPTER 18

Five Fields of Freedom

Alas, the procession comes to pass, memories will fade hopefully. And I can put this sordid affair behind me.

The ghastly eight horses hadn't fully reached their final destination.

Mr Freedom originated from Barcelona, Spain.

He still resides there today, in the same villa that he grew up in as a child with his parents. A childhood awash in parties, concerts and days spent cruising along the ocean surface on jetskis in sweltering eighty degree sunshine. No wonder his face seems factory-fitted with that broad smirk. In 1980, he sold his family's shares in Spanish Onions for a lot; when I say a lot, I mean an astronomical sum. And now Mr Freedom uses his funds to purchase rare, unique objects such as heirlooms, classic cars and superior thoroughbred racers.

The lorry floated up the highway. Vintage Red hummed along to the music flowing out of the speakers. A soothing unity swept the trailer. All these horses had spent years competing, sacrificing fun for the discipline of training, and now they could officially let their hair down.

"Give me an f," shouted Long Wait.

"F," they responded.

"Give me an r," she demanded.

"R," they gave.

You got it, those idiot horses went on to spell 'freedom', bravo.

"We're heading for the Channel crossing," said Heartbreaker.

Black Sheep, parading a healthier reduced muscle mass, feared the water. "I don't like the ocean."

"Why?" asked Vintage Red; he'd become a guardian for the others, sorting out squabbles.

"I can't swim."

Heartbreaker and Doo howled in laughter.

"We go by ferry. It's a giant boat," clarified Vintage.

Black Sheep calmed. In his defence he was new to international travel.

"I wonder what the Five Fields of Freedom have in store for us," said Something Good.

"As long as there isn't a jockey in sight, I couldn't give a flying duck," vented Black Sheep. The heavy whippings he'd taken had carved thick scars across his thighs.

"Oh, so won't you miss horse racing?" asked Long Wait.

"So long, see ya later, get out and don't let the door hit you," hollered Vintage Red.

Generally, all the horses shared Vintage's attitude, stuck in Something Good's thoughts he'd have dwelled on had he and Vintage contested the Chase authentically. Maybe something good could've transpired. A bittersweet taste of unfulfilled potential lingered. Mark my words, Vintage Red and Something Good will eventually clash. Not for now though.

The lorry breezed up to the docks, checking onto a cargo ship.

Safety regulations took an hour for them to clear. Usually for a bunch of supremely gifted horses, being shacked up in a cramped and humid space is deemed revolting. But not these irritating steeds, they chanted and chanted.

'Freedom, freedom, freedom,' maintaining rhythm.

"Where are you off to this fine morning, sir?" said the cargo inspector.

"Catalonia. Barcelona, in fact, my hometown," Mr Freedom said, beaming.

The inspector filled in a transfer paper for Mr Freedom, marginally put off by his fluffy attitude.

"Are you always so jubilant?" he wondered.

Mr Freedom folded the sheet into his jacket pocket. "Life's too short to be wasted unhappy, so smell the roses," he winked.

The inspector sauntered off, deciding Mr Freedom was utterly deranged.

Vintage and the gang eavesdropped to hear their new location.

"Viva España," said Something Good.

"Give me an s," said Long Wait.

"S," they bellowed.

Very good, they go on to spell Spain, hip, hip, hurrah, spare me the agony.

"Barcelona, has anyone ever been?" asked Long Wait.

"Once I raced in the Barcelona Grand Prix, won by a furlong," boasted Vintage Red.

Long Wait's tail flapped and a tiny twinkle dazzled her eyes when staring at Vintage Red.

"What were the people like?" questioned Heartbreaker, noticing the ferry slowing down.

"Gracious and honest," he claimed.

The lorry disembarked into Spain, and a considerable change in heat was noticeable. The truck coasted up the silky smooth Barcelona roads passing cathedrals, museums, incredible villas, the exquisite beach and the Nou Camp stadium.

"Almost there," squealed Nothing More, the bothersome leg mending rapidly.

The releasing valve on the lorry's air suspension had been activated. Bleep, bleep bleep repeated as it backed up the driveway. The locking handle tilted upwards and nine horses brimmed in heightened excitement. No, I didn't make a mistake, nine horses. Trailer doors sprung open as sunbeams soaked their coats. A heavy duty ramp was connected to the back.

Heartbreaker surged off first. He's such an adventurous sort. As the American strutted forward, a dozen giddy children bombarded him, tugging his tail and slapping his belly.

"Don't touch me there. I'm sensitive in that region," Heartbreaker squirmed.

The other seven steeds stalled; seeing the way Heartbreaker was pulled and pushed spooked them.

Mr Freedom had twelve glorious grandchildren. He'd do almost anything to please the little rascals. Their happiness inflated his own. So on weekends when they'd pop by, Mr Freedom brought a new toy for their amusement; today it was eight sensational thoroughbreds.

"I'm not a doll," said Heartbreaker, being consistently poked.

"Who's next?" Black Sheep asked.

They all hushed up timidly.

"You wussies, I'll go," Long Wait waltzed down the ramp. Her golden structure hypnotised the children.

"A golden one, she must be extraordinary." The dainty dozen charged at her, tossing Heartbreaker to one side.

"Fine, forget you then." Heartbreaker galloped away to view his fields of freedom.

Long Wait adored the little kids stroking her softly.

Vintage Red and co took their opportunity to slip around the back undiscovered. A hair-raising vision astonished the squad. Ritzy, rich, luscious, green fields spreading over a hundred acres were supported by heavenly and first-rate soil. Trees delivered areas of shade for when the flaming sun got too hot.

"Well, well, well," Something Good gasped. Those hellacious Siberian winter nights were now being melted in the sunshine.

"I'm in love," Nothing More blushed.

"I feel quite peckish," said Difference of Opinion, roaming into a stable. "Sweet, oats and corn, my favourite."

The horse pack retreated into the stables, fuelling up. Vintage Red stared into the navy blue ocean, quietly disenchanted.

A shadow trailed him.

"I'd know that walk anywhere," said an old friend.

Vintage's heart thumped. "Second to None! Old timer, you've landed on your feet here."

"I can't complain. I've forgotten what clouds are like."

"The sun definitely agrees with you, and the food," said Vintage Red, focused on his flabby tummy.

Second to None brushed his head against Vintage's neck, acknowledging how far they'd come. "We have a lot of catching up to do."

Vintage smiled. He knew Second to None was the only horse who had experienced his kind of lifestyle. "I bet you want to know how we ended up here."

"Of course. But first order of business, a race," stated Second to None. Four and a half years out of the game had left him eager.

"I'll humiliate you" Since Second to None's retirement, Vintage Red had gone from strength to strength.

"Back in Paris, if I'd sorted my start out you'd have lost son," replied Second to None, lying through his back, side and front teeth.

The horses smirked, lining up together.

"On my command," instructed Second to None.

"And what will that be?" asked Vintage Red.

Second to None leaped off, bolting from the stables. Vintage jogged, thinking his buddy needed the boost.

The steeds became trophy pets, living out their days in sunshine and luxury.

Until next time folks, bye from me and auf wiedersehen, au revoir, до свидания, さようなら, despedida from the Great Eight too.

FUN FACTS

- All thoroughbreds share the same birthday, either January 1st or August 1st

- Highest speed ever recorded by a racehorse was 43.97 mph by Winning Brew on May 14, 2008

- Most expensive racehorse ever was sold for $70 million

- The world's oldest regulated horse race is the Doncaster Gold Cup originally held in 1766

- The world's longest horse race is called the Mongol Derby, lasting eight days and covering an incredible 1,000 km (621 miles)

- The most prize money ever awarded was $20 million in the Saudi Cup

- The most money lost on one race is $2.3 million on a horse ironically called Essential Quality.

Printed in Great Britain
by Amazon

46795731R00079